The Seceret

The Seceret

Body Parts

David J. Dundas

iUniverse, Inc.
Bloomington

The Seceret
Body Parts

iUniverse books may be ordered through booksellers or by contacting:

iUniverse
1663 Liberty Drive
Bloomington, IN 47403
www.iuniverse.com
1-800-Authors (1-800-288-4677)

ISBN: 978-1-4502-7990-1 (sc)
ISBN: 978-1-4502-7991-8 (ebk)

Printed in the United States of America

iUniverse rev. date: 07/06/2011

Chapter 1

A Stranger in Town

He wandered aimlessly, almost in a catatonic state, unable to feel his own toes, his body stiff from the constant pounding from the weather. Yet he seemed oblivious and trudged on. The wicked wind seemed to penetrate his body, blowing him about the place like a rag doll. Pushing on, he vowed to himself never to return. The constant realization that he was leaving behind a horrible dream was good enough.

* * *

He had been so afraid when he left that he took only the clothes on his back. Now he felt faint as he pushed on. He felt his body go into overdrive, trying to jump-start his body. Feeling limp, he pressed on, determined not to stop. Whatever it took, he had to tell someone. He had to see a live person, someone, anyone.

Just then, slowly in the distance, he could see a vehicle coming toward him. The vehicle seemed to put him into a hypnotic trance. Could it be? Well, he was about to find out. He just stood there in the middle of the road like a dimwitted deer waiting to be hit by a vehicle. He stood there praying—no, begging—for the vehicle to end it all. At least he would not suffer any more. The dreams—oh, how they tormented him. He closed his eyes, waiting. *Damn,* he thought, *whatever was coming, was coming very slowly.* Wishing to end it all, he stood his ground as the distant beams of light got bigger and bigger.

The stranger, growing cold at the last minute, was having second thoughts. Yes, he was cold, hungry and scared but if he ended it all, who would warn the townsfolk? No, he had to do this, he thought, as he opened his eyes and continued to walk toward the light. Walking directly into the path of the vehicle, he started to flap his arms up and down, like an angry goose, trying to flag down the oncoming vehicle.

The driver of the vehicle was an over-zealous security officer. Yes, it was Oswald Peterson, a freckle-faced, all-American guy who did what he had to do to get through life. Yet on this wintry night all was to change. Yes, Oswald Peterson would not be the same. Oswald always dreamed of becoming a police officer, yet he always seemed to fall short. "C'mon, baby," he sang as he placed his foot against the accelerator. "You don't know," he bellowed. He hardly had time to react when he saw a shadow cast by the stranger walking toward him.

"Shit," he said as he slammed on the brakes. The vehicle seemed to cry at the very thought of the driver slamming it on so hard, and then glided as it swerved, almost artfully, just gently clipping the stranger. The stranger, upon seeing his life flash before his eyes, felt a sudden rush in him as his mind told his body to move, yet it was just a little too late. His reaction time was hindered due to the cold.

As the rusty station wagon came to a vicious halt, he heard, "Hey, mister, you all right?" The stranger could hear the distant, muffled voice, as he slipped into a state of unconsciousness. The weather and cold faded from his thoughts, and all the stranger could hear was, "Mister, hey, mister, you all right?" The stranger's eyes rolled around; his head was still chiming like bells.

"Hey, mister," Oswald barked. "Hey, you all right?"

"Where . . . where am I?" the stranger asked.

"Don't you know?" Oswald asked. "Hey, whose gonna pay for my ride?"

The stranger looked in the direction of the beat-up Volkswagen, now with steam emanating from the engine block.

"Look, don't get up," Oswald said. "You are very lucky. Hey, what's your game, man? Why were you walking out here?" The questions seemed to spit from Oswald's mouth.

But the stranger could only mutter, "I must go."

"Hey, buddy," Oswald said, "you're not going anywhere. The forecasters are calling for more snow, and your only hope out here is me."

"Well, I'm really screwed," the stranger said.

"Hey, watch your mouth."

"Look, no disrespect. I just have to get out of here."

"Well, it looks like we are both stuck!" Oswald pushed his seat back to reveal bags of junk food. "You hungry?" he asked the stranger.

The stranger did not respond but only looked at Oswald in astonishment. His one ride away from them, and now he was stuck; no, they were stuck.

"Look, all I want to know is why the hell you was out there. Where were you going?"

"My name is Michael, Michael Scott, and we need to get out of here."

"These here parts is my back yard. There is an old shack not too far from here. If you're up to it, we can hike it."

"Well, we can try," Michael said as they both watched the white smoke bellow from the engine. "Yeah, we can try."

The snow covered the entire area, including the skid marks the vehicle had made.

"We sure can't stay here," Oswald said as he clutched onto his bag of snacks. "Look, man, we can't stay here. We need to find that old shack"

"Yeah, I guess you're right," Michael said.

"See if this will fit," Oswald said as he tossed a worn jacket at Michael.

"Hey, thanks," he said.

"Thank me later," Oswald said. "The snow is not letting up, and we need to get you to a doctor."

"I am fine," Michael said. "I just need to get the hell out of this place."

"What place you talking about?" Oswald asked.

"I don't know."

"Wait a minute. You know your name but you don't know where you're going?"

"All I know is I don't want to go back."

"Hey, what's your story?" Oswald demanded.

"We just need to keep moving."

Oswald leaned forward and said, "You are the reason I'm stuck here. The least you could do is tell me what's going on."

From the stern look on Oswald's face Michael knew that his determination was their only chance of getting them out of the storm.

Oswald glanced down at Michael's foot and whistled. "Gee, mister, all I'm saying is that it is very strange to ever see anyone around here, and when I do, it's you—all busted up, and no shoes. What am I supposed to think?"

"All I can remember is my name," Michael replied. "I hope the rest will come to me."

"Yeah. Me, too," Oswald said. Oswald took his thick scarf from around his neck and tore it into two even pieces. "Put this around your feet," he told Michael.

"Thanks." Michael seemed shocked at Oswald's kindness; however, he had only one goal, and that was to leave.

"Hey, no problem," Oswald replied. "Listen, we have no means of transportation, so we must work this thing out together. So what do you say?"

"Let's do it," Michael said.

Oswald took one last look behind him, adjusted his jacket, and took a deep breath. "Yes, let's do it."

As they began the journey it seemed odd that a stranger, running from something mysterious, could find solace in another stranger.

Oswald found a large tree limb, sturdy enough to serve as a makeshift cane for Michael. "Here," Oswald said. "Take this."

"I appreciate your kindness."

"Don't thank me just yet," Oswald said. "On my way through, I saw an old shack. Maybe we can get us some help there."

"How far?" asked Michael

"Two, possibly three miles from here. Well, it would be if we were driving, but since we are legging it, stack another three miles onto that."

"Well," Michael said, "we won't get there if we continue to bicker."

"Oh, no one's bickering. It's just that, you know . . ."

"No, I don't," replied Michael.

"Well, my entire day was going great until I ran into you."

"Well, let's not forget how that happened," Michael replied.

They embarked on their long, arduous journey. As they trudged through the snow their journey finally looked like it was about to pay off. In spite of the blinding snow, which continued to punish them with every step, they detected a blur in the distance. They were almost there and Oswald shouted in glee.

Michael's feet were beyond feeling. All he could think about was experiencing the soothing sensation of heat as they slowly waded through the snow. It felt like they were slowly sinking in quicksand.

When they got to the house, it was hell clearing snow away from the front door. The door, still sturdy, was nevertheless well-worn like the rest of the house, which looked tired from years of neglect. The door knob was missing and the door had markings on it, probably placed by youngsters who thought it was okay to deface someone's house. It seemed a shame; this house had so much potential. The windows were coated with dirt and grime.

Any onlooker would think it quite strange to see these two grown men trying their very best to gain entry. Oswald made one last attempt to budge the tremendous door. Even though the door was riddled with dry rot, it was still sturdy.

"Shit," Oswald said. "Why don't we just bust a damn window?"

"Well, that would defeat the purpose," Michael said sarcastically.

Once inside the house it seemed dull, yet it had a certain ambience.

"Try to see if you can find something," Oswald said, "a candle, anything to help us see."

Oswald blindly felt his way toward a pantry. To his delight, it was stocked with canned goods.

"Hey, I found something," he yelled.

"What is it?" demanded Michael.

"Uh, pork and beans," he said with a chuckle. "Hey, this place is well stocked!" He continued to sift through as if he was feeling for gold. Just then he mumbled, "Dummy!" He rummaged through his pockets and pulled out his lighter. "Please don't fail me now." He repeatedly flicked the lighter with his nicotine-stained thumb. Finally the lighter gave in to his constant fumbling and a small flicker of light illuminated his pale freckled face. He pointed the small lighter with true aim toward the rest of the pantry. The light, however minimal it was, actually helped them in a big way, for in the corner of the pantry, directly under the old rusted sink, was an oil lamp. Oswald prayed that the lamp was filled. His prayer was answered. Oswald created a makeshift wick using an old boot lace. With this lit they were able to find some other goodies, including an old fireplace, which seemed to almost welcome them.

"Whew!" Michael said. "Heat!" His feet were slowly warming up.

"Boy, this ain't so bad," Oswald said coyly. "We got food."

"Hey, better check the expiration date on that."

"Relax," Oswald said. "We are good. Look, I don't know about you, but I'm hungry. No telling how long we will be here."

"You're right," Michael said.

"With the room lit by the oil lamp and with food in their stomachs, Oswald felt compelled to ask Michael what he was doing on that desolate road. He tried his best not to look at Michael's feet and he was a little surprised that Michael had not bitched about the discomfort he must be feeling. But he had to ask. He mustered enough courage to ask the stranger what, or whom, he was running from. He couldn't help but think that the stranger was hiding something, yet he thought it best keep this to himself. He looked at Michael's physique. He seemed quite athletic, but Oswald wondered how Michael had received the scar, which seemed too perfect, at the side of his neck.

"How did you get that?" Oswald asked, gesturing with his dirty spoon.

Surprised by the question, Michael quickly covered the scar.

"I'm sorry," Oswald said.

"No, no, it's not your fault. I'm just not ready."

"Well, it seemed quite strange that you was on that long dark stretch of road. It was just kind of spooky, you know?"

"Well, no, I don't," Michael said in his defense.

"Where were you coming from?"

"Look, I just can't tell you."

"Well," Oswald said, "when I saw you, you were very frantic. You were asking for the police. Well, buddy," Oswald said, "I am the closest thing to it. You sure you don't want me to know?"

"Huh?"

"What harm could it do, right?" Oswald said.

Michael took a deep breath. "You remember the Silvertown killings?"

"Shit, yeah!" Oswald said excitedly. "The serial killer. Yeah, sick puppy, sick indeed."

"Well, I was in town covering the story."

"Wait a minute," Oswald said. "When I saw you, you were not coming from Silvertown."

"No shit. You want to hear the story or not?" Michael snapped back. "Well, anyway, I was covering the story. All seemed quite the norm when I decided that I was hungry, so I did the next best thing. I took a slow walk down to the local diner. The crowd was very friendly, or so I thought. I ordered the rib special."

Oswald seemed to like the fact that food was mentioned; he seemed to salivate right before Michael's eyes. Michael went on only to be interrupted by the growl of Oswald's stomach.

"Sorry," Oswald said with an embarrassed grin.

"Well, anyway," Michael said, "I ordered my food. Nothing seemed out of place. The topic everyone was discussing was the serial killings."

Michael went on to describe each and every person in the diner. He started with the owner, a burly looking individual who did not talk much. All he said to his patrons was, "Eat up, plenty left."

* * *

People there were clearly close-knit, and Michael soon realized that they did not take kindly to strangers. Michael settled in to enjoy his meal and sensed a cold stare from someone in the room. But as he raised his head to enjoy a mouthful, all heads were turned away from him. Sitting adjacent to him, at the bar, was a female, very attractive apart from the flannel shirt and the oversized boots that she was wearing. All in all though, a decent lay. She had a long ponytail, which seemed to accentuate her girlish features. And she had freckles, which complemented her in every way. Michael had noticed her staring, but he was just passing through. However, progress toward his destination was hampered by the storm.

"You new to this place?"

Michael raised his head in disbelief that someone actually wanted to talk to a stranger.

"Yeah," he said as he wiped his mouth neatly with a sauce-stained napkin.

"We don't get many strangers around here so I must apologize for their interest in you when you came in. Where you headed?"

"Silvertown."

“Oh, that place,” she said. “Isn’t that where they had those murders?”

“Yes,” Michael said.

“Well, it’s a damn shame. Those innocent people . . . it just don’t seem right. I’m Doris,” she said, “Doris Fletcher.” She extended her hand to Michael.

“I’m Michael,” he said like a shy schoolboy. “Mike for short.”

“Well, Mike,” she said, “you got a last name?”

“Scott, Scott is my last name,” he stuttered.

“Well, enough of the formalities,” she said. “What brings you to good ole Larit? “Is that the name of this town?” Mike asked. “I was covering the town of Silvertown—you know, the killings—when I had a blowout, and here I am.”

“Yes, here you are,” she said with a look of admiration. “Well, don’t let me hold you up,” she said. “Your food is getting cold.”

Mike hurriedly gobbled up his food like a young child being scolded to eat his veggies.

* * *

“I remember washing my food down with a sweet wine,” Michael told Oswald. “It seemed quite rich, yet it was very pleasant going down. ‘Drink it all,’ the owner told me as he watched me swallow the last drop. ‘Plenty more left,’ he bellowed. At that point I felt almost sure that I was in a place like no other. Strange as it seems, I was right.

“Since I had no way of getting home to New York, especially in this storm, I had to settle for a fleabag motel. It was a seedy place with a vacancy light that flickered on and off and an exterior riddled with dirt, telltale signs of an unkempt place. I walked up to the front desk into a scene of confusion. I cleared my throat to get the attention of the attendant. ‘Excuse me,’ I said. ‘I’m from out of town, and would like a room.’ ‘You alone?’ a wiry voice asked. The clerk kept his back to me and I told him I was alone. ‘House rules: no whores, no noise, no trouble. I run a decent business here.’

“The clerk wore wire-rimmed glasses. His bald head was freckled with liver, and he had a whitish-looking beard, well kept. His teeth, which must have been white years back, were now yellow with fresh-looking muck on them. He crooked his finger and motioned for me to come in closer. 'Room 321, down the corridor, to the left. Just a reminder, lock your door,' he said, almost with a smirk. 'Lock my door?' I asked. 'Yes,' he said. 'Lock your door. We get many a drifter passing through, and by the looks of you, you ain't no drifter,' he said. I was mesmerized by the clerk's bony-looking finger and I tried my best not to look. I thanked him as he poked the key into my hands and then I walked gingerly toward my room. The hallway was very messy with bits of paper strewn all over the place. Man, what a shit hole! I fumbled my keys once, twice, and finally I was in my room. The room was quite normal, albeit filthy. Shit, I dared not sleep on the bed, so I took off my shoes and kicked my feet up onto the couch.

"All I remember is listening to a domestic spat. The walls seemed paper thin and a loud, coarse voice kept shouting, 'You fucking whore.' I could hear a woman sobbing unpretentiously. I almost felt sorry for her. Her sobs got louder and I heard a door slam. 'You get back in here!' the voice demanded. Then I heard her say, 'Drop dead,' and she walked slowly down the hallway. There was something very familiar about her voice and it finally dawned on me that she was the woman I had met earlier that day. I jumped up like an excited child, and slammed my left eye toward the peephole. Shit, it was her. I wanted to talk to her so bad—well, right then was not the best time. I mustered up enough courage to slowly turn the lock so I could go and console her. Yeah, right. Well, just at that same time her old man opened his door and lumbered out, looking at me with disgust. 'What the fuck you looking at?' he asked me. I said I was just getting a soda. Her husband seemed very threatening. I thought I could have kicked his ass on a good night, but probably not that night. He pushed himself toward me and ran outside to his woman. I could hear distant bickering. Then, as I heard the revving of an engine, he said, 'Turn it off, bitch.' 'No, leave me alone,' she cried. 'It's over.' And then I heard the loud screeching of tires and she drove off in an old beat-up rusty pickup, speeding off in a cloud of white tire smoke."

"Well, what happened next?" Oswald asked.

"Be patient," Michael said. "I couldn't wait to get the hell out of that fleabag motel. The night seemed to evaporate, and the morning sunlight was welcomed by the chirping of robins. Well it, seemed quite refreshing anyway. I hurriedly put on my shoes and threw some water on my face, paid my bill, and I was on my way. I was hungry so I thought I would visit the local eatery."

"The diner," Oswald uttered.

"Yeah," Michael said. "I entered the diner only to see the loud-mouth jerk from the motel. 'Well,' he said, 'if it ain't our local stranger.' I said good morning to him, trying not to make eye contact. 'Hey,' he said with a slight anger in his voice, 'ain't you that nosey son of a bitch from that motel?' I told him I didn't want any trouble. 'No problem,' he said. 'She left me.' 'She, meaning your wife,' I said. 'Yeah,' he said. 'Five years up in smoke. Bitch, she will pay,' he said as he swallowed his coffee and hurried out of the diner.

Chapter 2

Small Town, Big Secrets

"The day seemed very uneventful in the town of Larit," Michael said to Oswald, continuing his story. "The only buzz they had was when the press was passing through to Silvertown. The town was primarily a blue-collar town with a minimal crime rate.

"The waitress asked for my order and I said I wanted two eggs, over easy, toast and coffee. 'That all?' she asked me and I said, 'Yeah.' Then I said, 'Yes.' Funny how bad manners rub off on you. I thought everyone in the town had their heads up their ass. Well, that's their problem, I thought.

"All I could think about was getting back to New York. As I finished my last morsel I could see a small crowd gathering around, sort of like a bunch of squabbling hens. 'What's going on?' I asked no one in particular. One patron said it might be a fender bender; another asked why in the hell a fender bender would create such a fuss. I certainly had no clue but I was going to find out. I exited the diner and took my time to cross the busy street. As I came closer, all I could hear was, 'Is she dead? She's not moving.'

"I pushed my way through the crowd and it did not take me long to figure out who it was. It was Doris. Apparently, when her estranged husband said she would pay, he meant it. I never thought it would be like this. There, lying in the middle of the street—lying there like a discarded piece of junk—was Doris and she was dead. I stood there in the middle of the crowd. I watched the medical examiner place her gently onto the stretcher. She looked very peaceful, you know, just laying there. Whatever had struck her had done a swift job; there were no skid marks, no blood stains, nothing. Her vitals were taken on site, and then she was gone. It was so sudden. I thought to myself how strange it was for no one to have seen anything. The crowd, your average run-of-the-mill onlookers, quickly dispersed when they heard the distant sound of sirens. It looked almost comical to see them leave. It actually looked like cockroaches scattering when a light is turned on.

"I had nothing to run for so I maintained my stance and waited to see what the sheriff would do. The sheriff, a salt-and-pepper-haired individual, who looked like he was pissed off at the world, stepped out of his cruiser. 'What do we have here?' he asked as he towered over Doris, who appeared to be peacefully sleeping. The sheriff was the only one who believed in systematic micromanagement. He insisted on doing the job of three or even four deputies so he was always the first one on every scene, the last one to leave. He had to be involved in everything, no matter how trivial. Good old Sheriff Little was always there. He stood about 5'7" with a gut so large you would swear that he was pregnant, yet he seemed very militaristic. His tie pin glistened in the wintry weather. His shirt silently protested its daily stretch across his burly torso.

"'Hey,' he bellowed, 'this here is a crime scene.' But no one listened to him. He reached across the cruiser's steering wheel for the radio's microphone and requested more police officers. Soon the morning air was filled with the sound of wailing sirens and screeching tires. 'I want these here areas taped off,' he yelled as his deputies hurried around like frantic bees. 'What do you want?' he asked as he lumbered toward me. I said I didn't want anything, that I was waiting to cross the busy intersection and head back toward the diner. As I crossed the road I felt like I had a target branded on my back. I dared not look behind me for I knew it was the sheriff eye-balling me back to the diner.

"It all seemed very strange with the whole scenario behind Doris' death—her husband storming angrily out of the diner and four other witnesses who heard him say that she would pay. Yes, very strange. I headed on back, hoping to get my personal items and check on my vehicle, which had become lodged in an embankment. The weather was definitely not in my favor. I had no time to waste, for I had to get back to New York with this story from Silvertown but I felt there was something more to this sudden death of Doris, and with me being a investigative reporter—well, you know, a story is a story. I just couldn't help thinking that something was not right as I walked to where I knew my vehicle was. I did not think much of it until I finally realized that my vehicle was gone. All I saw was the trail it left. It was definitely gone, hopefully towed. I turned up my collar, and headed back toward Larit in search of my vehicle, still baffled by the demise of Doris.

"The news of the death of Doris had many people very upset. The fact that no one saw what had happened, the fact that her husband was missing, and the fact that it did not even make the town's newspaper seemed a little suspicious. I had all the time in the world to ponder this as I continued my trek toward the tow company. You would think a small town like Larit would at least have a taxi company. As I continued on, the weather seemed to at least break. The snowfall had somewhat subsided for now. As I continued to walk on, call it my being a regular New Yorker, but I felt like something or someone was behind me. I spun around—my eyes darted like a fiend's itching for a fix—hoping to see someone. 'Damn,' I said in frustration, 'this place is freaking me out.' Nothing was there, or so I thought.

"The town of Larit is generally a quiet town, apart from the hubbub from Silvertown, and people view the town as a gem. But it was hiding a dark secret; yes, something was wrong with the town."

"I don't get it," Oswald blurted out. "What happened to the husband? Did the cops investigate the homicide? Was it a homicide?"

"Hey, this is my story. Let me finish," Mike snapped. "Well, anyway, I was able to find the tow company, and inquire about the fees for storage and the initial tow. The garage was not so bad. It seemed well kept, and the owner was actually civil. 'Be right there,' a voice shouted from behind a rusty red Chevrolet. 'Please take your time.' The tow company's owner came to the counter and asked, 'Well, how can I help you?' I said I was there for my vehicle. 'Your vehicle?' the owner asked. He appeared to be puzzled. He looked quite educated, possibly a college flunky who fell short of getting the hell out of Larit. 'Yes, my blue Thunderbird, '72 edition, one of a kind,' I said proudly. He looked down at me with his wired specks. 'You might want to call Sheriff Little on that there vehicle,' he said in a weary tone. 'Look,' I demanded, 'all I want is my vehicle.' 'Look, son,' he said in a sarcastic tone, 'see this here release form? This here states that any vehicle involved in any town crime or a felony will remain on these here premises.' Upon hearing this, my ears started to ring like I had a personal choir boy ringing the shit out of my ears. *Crime or a felony.* I asked him his name. 'Don't you read?' he replied as he pointed toward his lower shirt lapel. 'Look,

Dan,' I said as I read it. 'Uh huh,' he said cynically. 'I am a reporter,' I continued. 'My car got stuck in the embankment, and I walked into town.' He broke in and said, 'Save your breath, son. You gotta speak with the sheriff. That's all I'm at liberty to tell you. I'd gladly call him for you.' I told him to go ahead. He reached for the phone, punched in the number and then said, 'Yeah, sheriff, it's Dan. You wanted me to give you a call if anyone came calling for the blue Thunderbird. Yep, uh huh, I'll let him know, sheriff.' He hung up the phone and said, 'Good news. Sheriff's coming to speak to you himself.'

"I did not know what all the fuss was but I waited and waited for the sheriff to show up. Finally he showed up. He had a very sinister look on his face. 'Can you tell me what's going on?' I asked. 'Look, son, I just need to ask you a few questions,' he blurted out. 'Can you tell me where you were the night of January 10 around 9:40 p.m.?" I told him I had checked in to the motel by the highway. 'From witnesses at the motel, you were the last one to see Doris alive,' the sheriff insisted. I said he couldn't possibly be insinuating that I had killed Doris. 'I am not insinuating anything,' he said. "Just calm down.' I told him I was calm even though I felt my pulse rising. I just wanted to find out what the hell was going on. 'You mind coming down to the station with me?' he said. I told him I most certainly did mind. I just wanted my car!! The sheriff took two steps back, and said with a sharp, demanding voice, 'Sheriff Little to central, send me a unit.' Within seconds the air was filled with the sound of sirens. 'I warned you, son,' he said. Before I could say another word, the sheriff took a can of police-issued mace and sprayed me. I dropped to the ground like a sack of potatoes, grazing my face. The burn was so intense that I jumped up instantly, screaming, 'Sir, I will do what you say, just don't spray me no more!!'

"All I remember is being led to a 5-foot-by-12-foot cell. I just could not fathom my fate, a big-city stranger in a small town. 'Wait a minute,' I said as I stood to my feet. 'What's the fucking charge?' Somebody yelled at me to pipe down. I jumped back and walked blindly toward the voice. 'Got a match?' the voice said. I fumbled through my pockets to give the stranger a light. He asked what I was in for. 'Dunno,' I said, 'they just said I had to answer some questions, and the next thing I was sprayed.' Commiserating, he said, 'Hurts like hell, doesn't it?' Then he asked where I was from. 'What's the deal? Why the questions?' I snapped back. The stranger said it seemed odd how I just came into town, and now I was in the slammer. That's all. The stranger was right. 'I'm just passing through,' the stranger said. There was something uncanny about the voice yet it had a familiar tone to it.

"As I tried to walk closer there was a rustle of keys. 'Hey, reporter boy,' one of the deputies said jokingly. 'Seemed your story checked out. Just sign here, and you will be out of here.' I scanned the forms quickly, and then I was escorted out to the main hallway, where I waited for the deputy to bring my belongings. I asked if someone could tell me what was going on. 'Look,' the deputy said, 'the less you know, the better for you; trust me.' The deputy was a youthful-looking person, early twenties. 'Just take your stuff, and leave,' he said.

"I was bent on finding out why the cloud of secrecy. 'Look,' the deputy said as he came closer, 'you remember the young woman, you know, Doris?' I told him I remembered her. 'Well, her body is missing.' I didn't know what to think. 'Missing?' I said. 'Didn't the coroner pick the body up?' The deputy said yes but that her body had disappeared.

"I realized that I could very well be on to something. I also knew from experience to get while the going was good; however, I had to ask one more question. 'Excuse me, deputy, there was someone inside my cell.' The deputy shook his head and said, 'That blast of spray must have messed you up. You were the only one in there.' I felt like I'd been hit with a sledge hammer. I felt my world turning like a carrousel. Doris' death, the thought that her body was missing, and people believing that I was a suspect made me want to get out of there.

"I hurried on with my clothes, grabbed the rest of my belongings, and hustled down the steps of the precinct. As I passed the door leading out, I realized I could hear the sheriff's voice. I overheard him arguing with someone over the phone. 'Damn it, I warned you! You never listen, do you. Now you will learn the hard way.' Just then he said, 'Hold on,' as he rose from his leather chair. He walked toward the door, made eye contact with me, and slammed the door. All I could hear was the muffled sound of him shouting at someone.

As I swung the front door open I caught glimpse of someone. It was a very familiar face. It was Doris' husband. He was across the road. I definitely knew it was him; those beady, penetrating eyes—it seemed like he wanted to tell me something. I stopped hoping to cross the busy street, but then his entire image was swallowed up by a passing bus. I told him to wait but by the time the bus had passed he was gone. Maybe he had some information? Anything was better than nothing. Yet it was just too late.

"As I turned up my collar, I couldn't help but think that this town of Larit was hiding something, and I was going to find out what. Yes, I would. As I crossed the busy intersection I had this very nervous notion that again someone or something was watching me. Maybe it was just a sudden case of paranoia, or was it? Yet I was certain that my being locked up and hearing voices was nothing but a clue. I had to regroup. I had to find out what happened to Doris' body.

"I decided to start with the morgue. Maybe, just maybe, I could find out what the hell was going on. Not wanting to draw any more attention to myself I continued my walk. I still had no real means of getting around; the sheriff was adamant about not giving me my vehicle back. He was almost sure that this vehicle—my vehicle—was the one used to kill Doris. Well, I knew one thing. Vehicle or no vehicle, I had to get to the morgue. I would never have thought that I would be in such a predicament, never in a million years. As I walked on, I thought about how the boys back in New York would get a kick out of this. Doris' demise seemed very spooky.

"As I continued to walk on the road, I listened to the sound of the slushy sludge of the wet snow as cars passed by. I tried not to walk too close to the curb for fear of being splashed. I was wondering what else could possibly happen to me. The weather at least was very good to me. The sun had even peeked through for a moment as I trudged on. I developed a kind of rhythm of getting out of the way of the gigantic puddles, which seemed to meet me with gaping mouths.

"As I waited for the traffic light to change, a black sedan pulled up to me. Being a New Yorker, I kept my head down and hurried my steps. I looked up, ready to bolt. The only thing stopping me was the warm friendly face that peered from behind the window. 'Hey, mister,' she said as my head spun around in amazement at her striking beauty. Her brunette hair seemed to welcome the wintry wind, which blew it gently across her face. She tossed her hair back and asked if I wanted a ride. With all the shit that was happening to me, I dared not get into the vehicle. But she was only being hospitable, or was she? Well, anyway, I took the ride."

"Well? Who was she?" Oswald rudely interrupted.

"Hey, I was just getting to that," Michael said. "She apparently remembered me from the diner. For all the tea in China I did not remember her. She said she was one of the waitresses working that day when Doris was apparently struck. 'Funny,' she said, 'I don't remember hearing anything—no tire screech—you know, nothing.' I couldn't help but steal a quick look at her alabaster skin and her reddish lips. Wow! A sure catch. From time to time she stole a quick glimpse at me and would smile very cunningly. She asked me for my name and, like a schoolboy on a first date, I stuttered my name. She said her name was Jenny MacCarthy.

"'Seems a shame what happened to Doris.' she said, and I agreed. 'So where you off to?' she asked. I suddenly mustered up enough courage to tell her I was trying to find the town morgue. 'Town morgue?' she repeated sheepishly. 'You have not had enough trouble? I told her that I just needed to find out what happened to Doris' body. 'Look,' she said, 'this is a small town and townsfolk, they really don't take kindly to you poking your nose around.' I told her I really respected that but there must be an explanation as to where her body is. 'Well, it's your funeral,' she said jokingly. I assured her that I didn't want to involve her and she asked me if I was some kind of cop. 'Me? No, I am an investigative reporter, so it's really my nature to kind of check things out,' I said. Smiling coyly, she said, 'Well, I guess it wouldn't do no harm in dropping you off. Just call it my good deed for the day.'

"The ride was just as pleasant as her smile. She wore a white shirt, which accentuated her slender torso. I couldn't help but fantasize how perfectly her nipples seemed. Her legs were very long and complemented her torso. She wore a pair of blue jeans that hugged her athletic figure. I followed her legs all the way up to her zipper region, which looked like a perfect camel toe."

"Fuck, yeah!" Oswald interrupted again.

"'Well, here we are,' she said. My fantasy came to a sudden halt. 'Please be careful,' she said. 'I know you don't know a lot about this town. I . . . I just don't want anything to happen to you,' she said. I said it seemed that I had a fan. 'Don't get beside yourself,' she said. 'You promise me you'll come back to the diner in one piece. Who knows what could happen.'

"I looked up at the morgue. It was rather picturesque with its trimmed rose gardens and neatly mulched flower beds. You could tell the place was well kept. I had no intention of sneaking around. I was to go directly to the front door, and sort of bullshit my way through. The door was an impressive sight; it was a seven-foot nicely polished door with a large black knocker in the middle of it shaped like a lion's head. I stood in front of the door feeling like a minute subject. I gave the door two very large knocks. To my surprise, the knocks seemed to echo throughout the house. I stood back and fixed my shirt collar, trying my best to look respectable. A short man answered the door. He looked almost like the British butlers I'd seen in movies. His balding head looked a mess; with so little hair, the comb-over was futile. I had definitely interrupted his work, whatever that was, for he was still wearing an apron and he had a look of bewilderment about him, as if to say, *What the hell do you want?*

"'Yes? Can I help you?' he asked. I told him my name but he said he knew who I was. Bad news travels fast, I guess. 'You were in the diner the day Doris died,' he said. I cautiously confirmed it. 'You see, this town really doesn't get newcomers, so when you drifted through, it was as if you brought bad vibes with you.' I told him that I was just passing through. 'Well, whatever,' he said rudely. 'How can I help you?' I told him that I was just trying to find out what happened to Doris. He interrupted and said, 'Look, a word of advice. We don't want your kind poking your nose around these parts.'

"I felt like a little child being scolded. It was almost enough to make me want to push my way past this person, who was in the way of my finding out the truth. But, no, I would wait. I did not care how long it took me; I would get to the bottom of this. I looked at the rude attendant and said I would leave. Before I had a chance to thank him, he slammed the door with a dismissive bang.

"I knew I was on to something. I would wait until it got dark. I would find out the truth, but I would wait until it got dark enough. I made sure he saw me walking away, only to slip off into the thick brush I had seen when I came there. I would wait until the time was right to make my move. It was definitely cold enough; the sun had cowered away from the brisk wintry air. I was definitely not prepared for this shit. The cold air seemed to run right through my bones. I felt like just packing it in and giving it up. I would have, too, if it had not been for the thought of Doris just laying there. I had to do this. The night sky seemed to slowly creep across the morgue, making the morgue look like a scary colossal structure, towering over its subjects. I could hear the calling of crows flying across the building, cawing as if to raise an alarm to alert all to my presence.

"As I snuggled closer toward the thick brush, my thoughts drifted to Jenny and her welcoming smile. I was able to relish the thought for only a brief moment. In the background, something or someone was slowly walking toward me. *Shit, this is it,* I thought. Well I was not going to go without a fight. I blindly reached behind me, fumbling for a loose tree stump. I pulled one close. I would give this son of a bitch a Babe Ruth clubbing. As the footsteps came closer, not caring if I was out there, I took a deep breath. But then a sweet voice yelled, 'Mike, no!' It was a voice that sounded so angelic yet reassuring that I was not the only jerk out in the woods. It was Jenny.

"'What the hell are you doing out here?' I whispered. She whispered back, 'I thought you might need this.' She reached toward me with a flask of coffee and some food. It was greatly appreciated. I downed the last bit of grub she had most graciously brought. She watched me almost proudly as I quickly devoured the food. I thanked her for the food as I used the bread to soak up the gravy. She said it was leftovers from the diner. 'I didn't want it to go to waste,' she said. 'Well, what did you find out?' I told her one thing was for certain; something was going on behind those walls. 'Michael, not to bust your bubble,' she said coyly, 'but there's always something happening. It's a morgue. I said I knew that but the pieces to the puzzle just didn't fit.

"'There you go again,' she hissed. 'I guess that that instinct of yours . . . 'I told her to be quiet. Then I grabbed her shoulders and pulled her close to the ground. 'Hey, watch your hands,' she said in a way to let me know that she was enjoying every bit of the action. I told her we'd be fucked if we got caught, especially me; I was not the town's favorite son. We both laid low and I could almost hear the beat of Jenny's heart. She was scared and I felt like I was her protector. I told her to move when I moved. I explained that I wanted to get as close to that basement window as possible. I cleared a small path through the thick brush. The brush felt like tangles of weeds. Pulling on them entangled their every move, hindering them from finding out the truth, the truth about Doris. I had begun to think that no one around there knew what was true.

"We quietly crept toward the basement window. The very thought of being caught made me realize that if I got caught I would definitely be fucked. But I kept my head down and whispered to Jenny to stay with me as we crept toward the basement window. What we were to find would change the outcome. The window was located right next to a fence, an old rickety fence that I had a hard time climbing over. I stepped up, placed my footing, and then thud! I fell to the floor with a loud *ooff!* Jenny said to take it easy and asked if I was okay. I whispered that I was fine but that this was a real test of my manhood. Then I saw how gracefully Jenny scaled the rickety fence. 'Show off,' I whispered. As we came closer to the window, we tried to pull the strands of weeds away from the window. The weeds seemed to have grown almost intentionally to cover the dealings going on inside.

"I finally pulled the weeds apart and could see a dim light, which seemed to be hanging on for dear life. In its flickering dim light I could almost see the silhouette of person lying there, waiting to be embalmed. But this room was different from any other rooms. It had a large stainless steel refrigerator that looked almost normal apart from the huge padlock on it. As we looked more closely, I gazed at Jenny. Her hair was pinned back, showing her youthful slender face. She looked back at me as if to give me a look of satisfaction. I looked around to see if the window could be budged, being careful to make sure that the window did not have an alarm. I moved my torso closer toward the window to try to pry the window open. Jenny watched my every move. Just then, as I slowly eased the window up, Jenny softly tugged at my jacket, easing me back. Shit, there was someone coming!!!

"The door slowly opened and the butler-looking guy, who had snubbed me so rudely, walked into the room. He had done this hundreds of times, yet he entered the room with the caution of a lion approaching its prey. He slowly walked toward the refrigerator, cautiously looking around the room as if something was awry. He looked toward the window. Jenny and I didn't dare to even breathe. He looked directly at the window, as if he was staring aimlessly into darkness. I shushed Jenny as the butler walked toward the window. Closer, closer he came. Just then the phone rang, throwing off the butler's concentration. This was definitely a blessing in disguise. I eased the window shut, and Jenny and I tried to figure out what to do next. We decided to wait. So wait we did until we heard the door to the colossal building slam shut. This was our chance to find out the truth. We watched the butler-looking individual get into his vehicle. This was our chance.

"I eased the window open, and we hustled to get inside. Once inside, it felt so weird. It had a putrid smell that took getting used to. We wandered around aimlessly, hoping to find something that would give us a clue as to what happened to Doris' body. We looked around the room with the light still flickering, and it seemed quite spooky. Jenny held my hand and I asked if she was okay. 'No,' she said. 'I only break into morgues on my day off.'

"As we continued the search, I was compelled to see what the hell was in that over-sized refrigerator. I asked Jenny to look around for a crowbar so I could get the fridge open. I walked slowly toward the fridge and Jenny handed me a hammer. I started to pry apart the thick chains. It was a good thing the butler had left because the noise I was making was loud enough to wake the dead. Jenny warned me to quiet down, but I asked who the hell I was going to wake up in a morgue. 'The dead don't joke around,' Jenny snapped back. 'This place gives me the creeps!'

"I finally pried the chain away. As the thick chains clinked to the floor with a rustic sound, it sent chills down Jenny's spine. 'Michael, can we go?' she asked. I told her to just let me see what was inside as I pulled the last chain off and opened the door of the fridge. A feeling of total disbelief came over me as I shuddered at the very thought of what was in front of me. Jenny said my name but I said nothing for I was in a total trance. 'Michael, what the hell is it?' she asked, her voice growing stronger. I told her I didn't know what it was. She walked up slowly behind me, and in the refrigerator were small parcels, all of which were labeled. Nothing strange, but the parcels were all oddly shaped and all labeled specifically for certain people, mostly people I had encountered in my little run-ins with locals. There was one labeled for Sheriff Little.

"'Mike,' Jenny said, 'this place is freaking me out. We just need to leave, and right now!' I told her I needed just one more minute, as I reached into my pants pocket to retrieve my little pocket knife. I just wanted to see what the hell was in the packages. I remember rummaging through the refrigerator as if I was in a grocery aisle looking for the ripest fruit. But this was different. Yes, indeed. I selected one with writing on it. Scribbled across the package was Sheriff Little's name. I took the pocket knife to gently ease it along the seal. Yes, I was going to get firsthand knowledge of what this town was hiding. I carefully placed the tip of the blade to the package. The contents inside the package started to seep through. I was so deep into uncovering what was inside that I did not notice the thick drops of blood emanating from the paper, drip by drip.

"Then it almost did not matter. I was suddenly talking to myself because, at the sight of the blood, Jenny had careened over, and was throwing up chunks of the food that we had eaten together. I tried to lighten the mood by telling her that she was making a mess. 'Funny, Mike,' she said. I told her that if I was right, I would be on to the biggest story since Sivertown. She asked me if that was all I cared about, just some story. 'What about Doris?' Jenny asked sarcastically. I told Jenny that if I was right, this package or packages are Doris. 'Pretty thin,' Jenny said. I told her to call it whatever she wanted to call it but that something stinks, and it wasn't just the morgue.

"'Wait, just wait,' Jenny said. 'These labeled packages? You mean body parts?' I told her that certain individuals apparently had a finicky taste for the obvious. I needed to get a few more names so I continued to sift through the refrigerator. 'C'mon, Michael,' Jenny said. 'I think I've had enough of this place.' As I was closing the refrigerator door, I happened to glance at the side door panel of the refrigerator and there, in plain view, was a tall glass-like container labeled 'diner.' With this I began to cringe at the very thought of munching down those vittles I so loved. And that red wine—nah.

"'Well,' Jenny said as she wiped her mouth, 'I am glad I am a vegetarian.' Easy for her to say. I told Jenny we should get the hell out of there and I slammed the door to the refrigerator. Jenny asked about replacing the chains, but I told her to forget about it. We hustled to get out of the morgue. Whew! That was not so bad. I helped Jenny out of the window and I could tell she wondered what I'd do about the morgue refrigerator.

"Jenny asked me what was next. I told her I planned to blow the lid off this whole thing. She asked me what proof I had of anything and I reminded her that we had a refrigerator load of body parts, with each part labeled to individuals in town. I believed I had a whole lot of evidence. But Jenny just wanted to get of there.

"'Poor Doris,' Jenny said. I could only echo what Jenny said. We quietly pulled out from behind the hiding place where Jenny had tucked away her vehicle. All seemed well; no one had seen us come or go, and no one would know that we had broken the law that night. At least that was what we wished for. We didn't realize that in the dark bushes a familiar face lurked, waiting—yes, waiting for the opportune moment but he would wait."

Chapter 3

The Blue Plate Special

Sheriff Little slammed down his phone with so much force you could have heard the tone chiming. “Get me Sullivan’s morgue on the horn right now, dammit.” The sheriff rubbed his chin nervously. “Seems like our friend was busy last night.” He gestured to himself. “Funny how accidents happen,” he said as he reached for the phone. He was to concoct a way to get rid of the stranger. No one was to find out, no one. He’d gotten away with this kind of thing for years. Now it was personal. His very existence as a sheriff would be at stake. “Hey, Miller,” he said on the other end of the phone. “Yeah, it’s me. It’s time to make good on that favor.” Then there was silence. What was the sheriff planning? It seemed more drastic than pinning a body on the stranger. “Yes,” he said as he picked up a clear bag. Across the bag it said evidence, and in this bag was a small item that Michael had left behind, apparently when he was making his exit with Jenny. In his haste he misjudged the placement of his pockets, and the knife had fallen on to the floor. With the butler-looking guy came in the next morning, he noticed many things awry, especially from the refrigerator. He picked up the phone and called the sheriff. Now the sheriff had the ball in his court, so to speak, and he called in a certain favor. He was to get the final say-so. “Oh, yeah,” said the sheriff. “My turn.” He tore open the bag and donned some latex gloves.

The news of the break-in spread throughout the town of Larit like wildfire. Any news was news, especially in a small town like Larit, a well-to-do town where everyone knew everyone else’s business, Michael turned over feverishly in his bed. He felt like he was in another world. He tried many times to comprehend the madness. Could the sheriff and his so-called cohorts be nothing but a bunch of flesh-eating, bone-sucking cannibals? *Perish the thought!*

Michael jumped out of his bed and performed his morning ritual of scratching his balls as he headed for the bathroom. As he washed his face, he couldn't help but wonder about Jenny and her innocent-looking face, bewildered by the find in the refrigerator. Mike quickly brushed his teeth, and headed out toward the diner. As he was exiting the room he knew that he had to watch his ass. He cautiously walked past the reception desk, where the attendant was busy watching the morning news. The attendant, however rude he was, turned from the television to see Michael walking out

"Hey there," he said cordially, "I made some coffee. Care to join me?"

Michael, surprised by the sudden invitation, remained stuck where he stood, and gently answered, "Sure."

The attendant gingerly pulled himself away from in front of the television, and walked over to the ready-made pantry area. He reached into the dusty cabinet, took out two dirty ceramic cups, and started to pour the coffee. He graciously handed the first cup to Michael.

"Thanks," Michael said warily, as he carefully watched the attendant pour the second cup for himself.

"Well, drink up," he said.

Michael cautiously raised his mug up toward his mouth, making eye contact with the attendant. With every motion, he hoped that the attendant would take the first sip.

"Ah, that's good shit," the attendant said as he slurped the coffee. His stained teeth told a story of years of neglect, and of time taking its course. His wire-rimmed glasses seemed to give his face more character, tempered somewhat by the grayish hairs protruding from his nose.

Michael dared not take a sip for this was quite awkward. "Well, I have to be going now," Michael finally said.

"You checking out?" The attendant asked, sounding surprised.

"Err, no," Michael said instantly. "I've decided I will stick around for a few more days."

With this he crooked his finger for Michael to come closer. He looked at Michael with an intense glare. "You heard about those morgue break-ins?"

"Break-ins?" Michael asked innocently.

"Yeah, strange things have been occurring lately," the attendant said.

"Well, I have to go," Michael said as he hurried out of the motel's lobby. Wishing that he had not taken that invitation from the attendant, he fumbled through his pockets and walked directly over to the public phone, which was adjacent to the motel. Once inside the phone booth, he unfolded a piece of paper. The number on the paper was hardly readable due to the sweat from Michael's trouser pocket, yet he was able to slowly decipher the numbers on it. It was Jenny's phone number. He thought if anyone could help him, it would be Jenny. He started to dial the phone number, his cuticle-riddled fingers aching as he pounded out the number. Then he waited for the phone to ring on the other end.

Jenny had had enough theatrics for the night, and had decided to call in sick. It was a good decision. The diner was very busy that day.

As the owner churned meat through the grinder he yelled to the busboys to hurry up and clear the table. He was preparing a special meal today, compliments of the sheriff. You see, Sheriff Little's word was gold in the town of Larit, and whenever Harvey's good ol' diner needed meat, Sheriff Little would surely oblige, no questions asked. He was just surprised at how the townsfolk would line up early in the morning, their mouths nearly salivating, and almost everyone would order the same thing: meatballs, with extra meat. He chuckled at the very thought of how his business was booming. Today he was serving the house special: broiled ham hocks accompanied by the house special red wine sauce. Not for one moment did he ever question the sheriff, not once. Yet all they had in common was money. Oh, yes, the sheriff cared about supply and demand. If he was supplying the meat, good ol' Harvey would give him a kickback. *Just a little, greedy bastard*, Harvey thought to himself as he wiped the sweat away from his brow, not caring if a droplet fell into his little mix. "C'mon, fellas, get the lead out," he yelled. "Hey, did anyone call to check up on Jenny?" he yelled as he continued to concoct his little house special.

Jenny was busy at home trying to tie up a few loose ends. If memory served her right, she was witness to something truly horrible. You see, Jenny the second-youngest out of five, was the only one who had decided to hang in and stay in Larit but after what she had seen, she was hightailing it out of town. She felt a slight bit of remorse for not hooking up with Michael. She thought that he could have actually been Mister Right.

She had been in quite a few relationships that started out with a spark, and then ended with a fizzle. Yes this town girl had definitely had her share of men who quickly left her after they found out that she could not get pregnant. Not by her choice. She had met this Texan who thought the only way to communicate was by using his hands, and unfortunately she fell victim to his abuse. He struck her once too often in her stomach. Still, she thought to herself, one day she would meet her Prince Charming, and he would take her away from this hellhole they called Larit.

The phone continued to ring as Jenny debated whether or not she should answer it. *Screw it,* she thought. She grabbed the rest of her belongings and headed for the door. As she opened her door she suffered a swift blow to her face. You see, the sheriff had called in a favor. And Miller was to make good on it.

Miller was the town's troublemaker, always in and out of trouble. Still, the only one who saw potential in him was the sheriff. And the sheriff had his own agenda, which included revenge and blackmail. Why Jenny? Why not? Since Michael had blown through town, Jenny was the only one who had helped him out, so to speak, so the stage was set and Miller performed his good deed for the sheriff. Miller licked his lips as he looked down at Jenny. As he knelt down, he could see her chest rising, however slightly.

"Shit!" he said. "The sheriff said nothing about killing anyone."

He scrambled to his feet in complete fright, and bolted through the door. Poor Miller. He was just a low-level punk with no direction, very easily misled, just the way the sheriff liked it. Miller got behind the wheel of his '78 pickup truck, and the tires spun around violently as he tried to make a quick getaway, only to lose control of his pickup truck and wrap it around a tree, Upon making contact, the truck became engulfed in a thick cloud of smoke. Miller, who totally panicked, was unable to escape. All that could be heard were his agonizing screams for help.

"Ouch!! That must of hurt," the sheriff said as he looked on. *Well, too bad for Miller,* he thought. That was one less witness he had to dispose of. He backed his vehicle out from behind the trailer park and disappeared as if nothing had occurred.

Michael continued to wait, hoping that by some small miracle Jenny would answer. “Shit,” he said as he slammed the phone down with great discontent. He had a gut feeling that something was not right. Indeed, he was sure that something had happened to Jenny. He was to find out, but how? He had no ride because the sheriff still had his vehicle impounded. I guess that that was the sheriff’s way of showing outsiders not to fuck up, especially in Larit.

* * *

“So what now?” Oswald asked.

“Well, I did what anyone in my shit would have done,” Michael responded. “I stole a car. Once I had wheels, I started thinking about a lot of unanswered questions out there, like what happened to Doris’ husband? How can people just vanish like that? I felt like I was stranded with no help. The only help I had was not answering her phone so I headed for the only place where I might at least get some answers, the diner.

“As I entered the diner I had this overwhelming feeling that I was going to throw up. I walked past a customer who was eating spaghetti. The sight of the red sauce had my stomach churning like butter in a vat. *Good luck, pal,* I thought to myself as he slurped up his spaghetti.

“‘Hey, there’s seconds for anyone who wants it,’ Harvey said.

“The muffled chattering in the diner seemed to rise a notch at the very mention of seconds.

“‘Excuse me,’ I said as I stopped one of the waitresses. ‘I’m a friend of Jenny’s. Is she here today?’

“‘Jenny called in sick today,’ the waitress said as she swerved around me like I was just a median invading her passage.

“‘Called in sick?’ I asked.

“‘Yup. You having yours here or to go?’ the waitress asked without making eye contact.

“‘Oh, just a coffee to go,’ I said. ‘Listen, I was wondering if you could help me out with something. I really need to get in touch with Jenny.’

“‘You want her phone number? the waitress asked.

“I told her I already had it and said I just needed her home address.

"'Look,' the waitress said, 'we don't normally do this but you're kinda' cute. Well, here it is.'

"I thanked her, paid for the coffee, and hustled out the door.

* * *

Harvey asked the waitress what Michael wanted and she said he was just passing through.

Jenny was still feeling the sting from the sucker punch that Miller had given to her and she barely managed to pick herself up off of the floor. Her lily-white shirt was drenched with blood from the barrage of punches she had received from Miller. She felt the blood rush straight to her head and lunged forward, smashing a table lamp into many perfect pieces, sending them all over her floor like little white fleeing gnats. She managed to regain her balance, and then proceeded as if in a drunken state toward the bathroom, both hands out to break her fall.

Once she was able to get inside the bathroom, she blindly searched around for the light, which was nothing but a white string attached to a metal coil. She pulled at it and with each tug she winced in pain. Finally the light came on. She looked at herself in the mirror. The reflection seemed to paralyze her, for she just stood there gazing into the mirror. She used her hands to gently parted her hair, which was clotted with her own blood. She turned on the water faucet, and then gently placed her hands into the lukewarm water. The warm water provided a welcome sensation.

Just as she reached for a towel, there was a distinctive and annoying tap on her front door window. *Tap, tap.* Fearing it was Miller returning for a second go at her, Jenny reached for the light, almost knocking herself out in the process. *Tap, tap.*

Then Jenny heard a voice she knew.

"Jenny, Jenny, are you in there?"

Jenny almost pissed in her pants as she cautiously hobbled from the bathroom to the rear door,

Tap, tap.

"Jenny!!" The voice got louder.

Yes, it was Michael. She scurried to unlock the door, and then quickly opened the door. Michael stood there, horrified.

"Those bastards," he said as he gently comforted the sobbing Jenny. He felt the closeness that they shared, and he whispered to her, "It's ok, it's ok." As their eyes met, Michael couldn't help but gaze into her eyes. The mascara she was wearing had created long streaks streaming down her face.

She looked up and said to Michael, "Promise me you will take me with you." Michael, who was a sucker for a pretty face, gazed back and promised.

The news of the Miller car crash had saddened the entire community. At his memorial service his family made sure that he had a closed casket. Many people filed past the simple coffin. His family, well respected in town, all sat in the front row, and gave a perfunctory nod to everyone who filed past the coffin, trying not to make eye contact with any one of them. There were many long, drawn-out speeches until Sheriff Little walked up to the podium, donned a pair of half-moon specks, and systematically cleared his throat so as to reaffirm his authority in the room.

"When I first met John Miller, he was nothing but a young juvenile delinquent, a real know-it-all," Little added. "John Miller would have given you the shirt off his back. Yeah, he had his share of run-ins with the law, but he was still a human being. Now I guess he will be making his final peace with his maker."

With this the sheriff made his exit. The townsfolk seemed to be in awe of his brief, yet subtle speech. His presence there would serve as the perfect alibi, especially if that nosey son of a bitch reporter suddenly catches on to his actions. *Yes,* he chuckled to himself, *your move, asshole.* With Miller out of the way, he would be able to hide another body, which happened to be the body of Doris's husband. Apparently, the sheriff had been very busy indeed. Not to pat himself on the back—he was just tying up all loose ends and no one would stop him. No one!! So what if he dabbled in human delicacies? *What's not to love,* he thought. He first experienced the taste of human flesh when he and some infantry buddies got stranded on an island off Laos and he did what he had to do to stay alive. Having Michael running around there like a crusader with a cause made him fucking sick to his stomach.

The sheriff slowly got into his cruiser, debating his next move. His next move was to issue an APB—an all points bulletin—for Michael's possible involvement in the recent bizarre killings that had started to plague the town of Larit. With this he snatched the hand-held radio from his cruiser and asked dispatch to patch him through to the state police. He figured if his little plan did not work, at least he would have another agency in town to take the heat.

Michael tried his best to suture the wound Jenny had received at Miller's chubby hands. He could have easily cut his losses, and jumped on the turnpike back to New York City, yet he felt compelled to stay and weather the storm with Jenny. He had been in small jams before but nothing like this. *Oh, no,* Michael thought to himself, *this was definitely one for the record books.*

"Ouch," complained Jenny.

"Look," Michael said, "you have a little cut that needs to be looked at."

"Well, you're no doctor," Jenny replied, sounding ungrateful.

"It's not much but this will at least stop the bleeding," Michael said.

"Hey, not bad," she said as she gazed back at herself in the mirror still not happy with what she saw. "Bastard," she said.

"I assume you're talking about that son of a bitch that tuned you up," Michael responded.

"Yeah, Miller," she said.

"Well, he must have shit his pants when his truck went out of control and wrapped itself around that oak tree."

Jenny gazed back at Michael with a regretful look on her face. "I did not mean that," she said.

"I'm sure you didn't," Michael added. "What we need to do is get the hell out of this town before the body count rises."

"What do you mean?" Jenny asked.

"Just look," Michael said as he motioned her to turn her attention to TV. It was on but the volume was down.

"Can you turn it up?" Jenny asked.

Michael turned up the old-fashioned knob on the TV. There was an attractive female reporter, dressed very professionally. And her surroundings looked very familiar. Jenny slowly walked toward Michael's blind side and slowly sat down by the front of the bed as they both listened intently to what the reporter said. In a somewhat childish voice the reporter started to describe her findings and questioned a passerby as to whether he knew the victims who were found brutally slaughtered.

Simultaneously, Jenny and Michael said, "What the . . . ,"

In mid-sentence Michael said, "This just is not right. We need to fix this.

"Listen to me," Jenny said.

"No!!" Michael said. "We need to leave, and right now."

"Leave, and do what?" Jenny asked. "And be on the run like fugitives? We need a plan. We need to sit and plan," she said.

"Plan?" Michael asked. "I guess you did not hear what the reporter was saying. They are looking for me! Not you, me! Me, god dammit."

Jenny rose up in bewilderment and slowly started to back away from Michael in disbelief.

"Jenny," Michael said, "I am sorry. I just need time to think this over. The sheriff is just trying his best to sink me at every chance he gets. Why me? There is only one thing we can do." Michael held Jenny's hand and they sat down to draw up a plan to get Michael out of the jam he was in and give the sheriff a dose of his own medicine at the same time.

Chapter 4

Hide and Seek

News about the murders spread around the once-so-peaceful town of Larit. It seemed that with the involvement of the state police, no stone would be left unturned. The townsfolk of Larit actually felt like local celebrities, albeit with a negative cloud looming over their heads. There was a killer on the loose. The lifestyle of many townsfolk had changed drastically. The sheriff made sure of that with his melodramatic TV interviews. How easy it was to pin the murders of numerous townsfolk on Michael. It was oh, so easy. And with the state police busy doing their door-to-door interviews, the sheriff was left to do as he pleased.

The state police special crimes unit was made up of two investigators, one a butch female named Chris Taylor, a seasoned vet, who was well known throughout the force as a ball buster. Her partner, Investigator Dwayne Mullins, was a nerdy trooper who had generally mastered the technique of forensics. Taylor was now the lead investigator. She sat down behind the small desk that Sheriff Little had so graciously provided, and munched on a cold piece of toast.

"What have we got?" Taylor asked her partner.

"Well," Mullins said, "we have numerous victims presumed dead. Or at least that's what we got from the sheriff."

"Is that so," Taylor said with a hint of discontent. "Funny, it's like the town sheriff just threw this entire mess into our hands."

"Well, what else would you do?" Mullins said in the sheriff's defense.

"Look, Mullins," Taylor hissed back, "when will you see the big picture? There is more to it than just plain missing people."

"What are you saying?" Mullins snapped back.

"All I'm saying is that after years on the force and hundreds of collars you just don't take anything at face value," Taylor said.

"Yeah, but!" Mullins interrupted.

"But nothing," Taylor replied. "How much time do you have on the job?"

"Well, I'm in forensics," he said proudly.

"This I know," Taylor said as she shook her head. "This I know."

The buzz about the state police being in town spread through the town like wildfire. The press was having a field day.

Sheriff Little read that one statement called for outside help. Another said the body count keeps rising." The frenzy was on, and this was just what the sheriff wanted. He wanted to create a diversion to keep the heat off him while he tried to find out where the hell Michael was. Yes, he was going to find him and kill him. But it was like Michael had just fallen off the planet.

"I should be so lucky," the sheriff said to himself with a chuckle.

You see, the sheriff had to make his move now. He had to find that son of a bitch. His retirement was starting to look even better. He picked up his walkie-talkie and called into headquarters.

Michael continued to peep through Jenny's cracked window. He felt like he had to get out of Larit, and quickly, but not without sending Sheriff Little a *fuck you very much.* He sat intensely biting his nails. Then it dawned on him that the only way to deal with a snake like the sheriff was to deal dirty.

He reached across and gently touched Jenny on her shoulder. Jenny seemed like she was still pissed off from Michael going off on her earlier.

"Uh, Jen," he said as he tried to cheer her up. "You got a bite to eat?"

"Sure," she said as she got off the bed.

He felt sorry for the way he had acted. He felt like a jerk and he knew she was still pissed off because she made no eye contact with him when she said sure. *Wow! I guess this was what it was like to be in the dog house.* He followed her to the kitchen and stood by the door entrance.

"You need some help?" he asked innocently.

"No," she said softly.

"Look, I know you don't have to do this."

"Do what? she asked.

"You know," Michael said. "Help me out." Michael's voice revealed his frustration.

"Well, it's not like I can just snap my fingers and have dinner appear," she said sarcastically.

"I know," Michael said.

"Michael, ever since I met you my whole life has changed. I can't say that it has not been different."

"How different?" Michael interrupted.

"Well," she said, "I am now a fugitive."

"Well, not exactly," Michael said. "The sheriff thinks you are dead. We have him by the balls, Jenny. Imagine what would happen if you just turned up at work?"

"What about the cut?"

"Screw it," Michael said excitingly. "Just say you slipped."

"Well, I guess it could work."

"You bet your sweet ass it would work."

"You want butter on your toast?"

"Got jam?" Michael asked.

"Sure," she said as she reached to open the pantry door. As she reached, Michael gazed at her body, which was symmetrically perfect.

"You . . . um . . . think we could . . . err," Michael clumsily asked.

She looked away from reaching for the jam and her eyes met Michael's. He leaned away from the door and started to slowly walk toward her.

"You were saying?" she said to Michael.

"I, I said do you think this will work?"

He continued to walk closer to her. She stood motionlessly with her hands around the jam.

"Could you help me with this?" she asked softly.

"Sure."

As Michael placed his hands on hers, she felt his breath. As he stepped closer, he watched as her chest started to rise slowly. He gently moved her hair aside, and placed the open jam on the counter.

"Tha, thanks," she stuttered as he coolly responded that she was welcome.

Jenny started to nervously bite her lower lip as Michael turned again and walked toward her. He was so close that she felt the hardness of his cock pressed against her.

She gently said, "I, I can't look. I don't want to send any signals.

"Well," Michael said, "message received."

He placed her hands on his cock. As she felt his manliness and swooned in ecstasy, he gently unbuttoned her blouse. Her breasts were perfectly sized as they protruded through her lavender lace bra. Her nipples, neatly erect, stood at attention like toy soldiers in a procession. As he gently followed the seam of her bra, Michael felt like a king as he felt her melting slowly into his arms. He started to unhook Jenny's bra. Well, at least he tried. He pulled and pulled—it was kind of a mood killer—before Jenny unhitched the bra without missing a beat. As they continued to kiss, Jenny felt her pussy dripping like a honeydew. Yes, she had not felt like this in years. Her pussy was slippery like a sticky mango as he guided his fingers gently over her rock hard nipples and then toward her spot, slowly peeling back her white cotton panties and slowly guiding his nose close to her spot. He thrust his long tongue, gently caressing her pussy.

Jenny screamed in total amazement. "Shit!!" she gasped as she looked down to see Michael's head buried in her cunt. "Yes!" she screamed. "Yes!" She lay back on the counter ready to receive Michael.

I got her now, Michael thought as he unzipped his pants.

* * *

Trooper Taylor pulled into the parking lot of the diner. She was there to meet Trooper Mullins. The weather was cooperating and the sun revealed its rays, momentarily casting a semi-warm look to the town of Larit. The town seemed almost normal with the constant flow of customers entering the diner.

What was so special about this place? she wondered. *Must be the friendly service.* Well, that's what she wanted to think. She slowly sipped her coffee, so as not to burn her lips. Then there was a tap on the blind side of her cruiser. "What the . . . ," she said as she jumped back, trying to guide her coffee away from burning her lap.

"Hey, Taylor!" Mullins said.

"You asshole!" Taylor screamed.

"Hey, boss, you got to try the meatballs," he said like a kid discovering a new toy.

"Meatballs this early?" she asked as he got into the cruiser.

"Yeah, and it's great," he said. "I don't know what's in this sauce but it's terrific."

He was devouring the food and unwrapped a roll so he could place a piece of meat inside the roll. He took a big bite. Then Mullins started chewing. As he chewed, Taylor looked at him in total disgust. The sauce trickled slowly down the side of his mouth.

"Hey," Taylor said, "take it easy."

"You sure you don't want any?" Mullins asked as he shoved the food near her face.

"I said no."

As Mullins took another bite, he winced in pain.

"Hey, Mullins, you OK?" Taylor asked.

"Yeah," he said as he slowly sorted through his food, as if he had a fish bone in his mouth.

"What is it?" she asked.

"Dunno," he said. He reached for his white napkin and cautiously brought the napkin to his mouth, retrieving something. It looked familiar. It couldn't be!

"What the fuck is that!!" Taylor asked.

"You tell me."

"You were eating it," she said.

As Mullins wiped away the sauce and the bread crumbs it seemed to be staring at him. It was an eye, and not just any eye. It was a human eye. Upon seeing this, Mullins doubled over and started to vomit violently.

"What did I tell you?" Taylor asked confidently.

"Never take anything at face value."

"Fuck me," she said. "Body parts. Yeah, body parts. It all adds up. The body count, the missing people."

"Wait, you're losing me," Mullins said.

"Listen," Taylor said, "that Sheriff Little—yeah, that bug-eyed son of a bitch. Call it intuition but he's dirty, dirty."

"I don't understand," Mullins interrupted.

"Why would he call for outside help? A small town like this, throwing out the welcome mat—why now?" Taylor added.

"Yeah, why now?" Mullins said with a quizzical look on his face.

"Look," Taylor added, "I need you to get this to the lab as soon as possible."

"Well, I have something better than that," he said as he dove into his bag. He might be a computer geek but he knew his way around forensics. He grabbed a small Petri dish and smeared the eye back and forth. Then he took a cotton swab attached to a long stick and gently poked the eye.

"You're a sick man," Taylor said.

"I will get this to forensics," he said.

"Hey, make sure you clean this up," Taylor said, pointing to his vomit.

"Yes, ma'am," he said sarcastically.

"And make sure you check in with me in a timely fashion."

"I will keep you posted in reference to my findings," he said.

"Watch your ass, Mullins."

"Sure," he said. "But I'd rather watch yours."

"Wiseass," she said as she watched Mullins walk back over to his cruiser.

This finding gave Trooper Taylor a fresh perspective. Surely something was wrong, she thought to herself. The first thing she had to do was interview the sheriff and watch his body language. She had to be very careful. The sheriff was no slouch and he would definitely have his guard up. Yes, indeed. The only good lead was the eye that Mullins almost gagged on. It sickened her to think that something like this could happen.

Taylor cautiously adjusted her rearview mirror. Something was wrong, she thought, terribly wrong. She knew that Mullins was not in the least a street-oriented cop. Shit, he was a pencil pusher. With all the other troopers tied up on other cases she was all he had, and all they had was each other. She started the engine to her unmarked Crown Victoria. The engine roared like a caged lion as she fumbled for her cell phone to call Mullins. Just a quick check on him. *This does not feel right,* she thought to herself as she backed her vehicle out of the diner's parking lot.

Back at the police station Mullins, still feeling a little nauseous, quivered at the thought that he had sampled human flesh. It seemed a little spicy. As he reached for a toothpick he shook his head in disbelief, wondering if he was the only one going through this. *For one thing,* he thought to himself, *this case is going to be solved.* He sifted through the files of all the missing people and started going through them in alphabetical order. *Dead or missing, some of the victims must have some sort of next of kin,* he thought to himself. He continued to go through the files; however, it seemed that all information leading to the family had been removed. He found this most odd. *Why?* he thought to himself as he continued to go through the files. All of the information referred to the town morgue. Hmm. Town morgue. It seemed very strange that all of the victims' families had given up hope of ever finding their loved ones.

He cautiously unraveled the eye from the paper napkin. The DNA kit would have been most helpful but how can you use the test kit, when there is no point of contact in reference to family? *Dead end,* he thought to himself.

His cell phone vibrated, alerting him to a call. "Yeah, boss, right away," he said in anxiously. It was Taylor. Apparently she had a hunch that a good lead could be found at the local morgue. "Well, at least you got something," he said to himself as he ended the call.

Taylor was certain that something had to start from the morgue. She was still very confused at the fact that the sheriff seemed almost happy with their presence. Yes, something was wrong. She pulled her vehicle into the lot of the morgue, almost wishing that they could find something, anything, to bring closure to the bizarre happenings in Larit. If any time was right the time was now.

* * *

Jenny slowly pulled the white sheets from the bed and wrapped herself. She was still dazed at Michael's performance from the previous night. She had not felt like that in years. She felt sort of liberated. As she climaxed, she slowly felt herself leaving all of the excess baggage behind. She gently eased herself into her fluffy slippers. Michael was still asleep. She watched him sleep. He looked very peaceful lying there.

She just wanted out of this mess. Her sense of hopefulness was tempered somewhat because Michael was now a wanted man on the run. She walked over to the phone in the kitchen and dialed. The phone rang on the other end, and then she heard a very familiar voice. It was her coworker.

"Yeah, I'm alright," she said. "Uh huh. Where am I?" Jenny repeated. She was still too cautious of who might be at the diner.

"Are you home?" the voice asked.

"No," Jenny said defensively.

"Well, where are you?" the voice asked carefully.

"I, I will call you later," Jenny said in a frightened tone. "I have to go," she said as she hung up the phone, not knowing that someone was listening on the other end.

Yes, how he listened very intently, cautious not to miss a bit of information. The sheriff chewed on the end of a soggy toothpick. *Shit,* he thought to himself, *that bitch is still alive.* Sheriff Little thanked the elderly phone operator, and then made a quick exit.

Jenny, fearing that she had screwed up, quickly started shaking Michael. "Mike! Mike!" she said as she continued to shake him. "Wake up!"

"What!" he said annoyed.

"We have to leave, and right now."

"Wa, what happened?" Michael asked, still groggy from his sleep.

"I, I called the diner," she said, bursting into tears.

"Hey, now," Michael said as he tried to console her. "It can't be that bad."

"You don't understand," she said.

Then it clicked. "Sheriff Little!" he said. "Quick."

They hustled together trying to pack what little clothes they could into a duffel bag.

The heat was definitely on the sheriff. He knew he had screwed up. He knew for one that Miller did not finish Jenny off as he requested. Here were the only two people who could tie him to the mess that he had created. *Not by choice,* he thought. The sheriff was driven by pure greed. Body parts had made him rich, and now he was not going to let a whore and a nosey reporter end it for him. "Not just yet," the sheriff said to himself, "not just yet." He knew that the state police were on a wild goose chase, and if that nosey son of a bitch reporter showed up, he was as good as dead. Yes, the sheriff had calculated every move but this one.

Knowing that Jenny had placed a call from her home gave him a warm feeling inside. Maybe he'd fuck her before he snaps that pretty neck of hers. It almost made him salivate, wondering how sweet her flesh must taste. The sheriff was definitely on a mission, and no one was going to stop him.

Trooper Mullins pulled into the parking lot of the morgue alongside Taylor.

"What took you so long?" she asked.

"I got lost," Mullins said cynically.

"I bet you did," Taylor said sarcastically.

"What you got?" Mullins asked.

"I think we should start from here," Taylor said.

"Why the morgue? Mullins asked.

"I think we can find whatever we are looking for in here."

"Well, you're the boss," Mullins said.

"Yeah, and don't you forget it, fish eye."

"Fish eye?" Mullins said. "Low blow. A man can't chew on a human eye without getting his balls busted."

"Hey get the lead out," Taylor said as they exited their cruisers.

"Don't we need a warrant?" Mullins asked.

"Warrant?" Taylor said in disgust. "The only warrant we need is this. She opened her jacket and showed Mullins her sidearm.

"That's not departmental issue," he said enviously.

"Yeah, and who's going to find out?" Taylor said in her defense.

"What the hell is it?" Mullins asked.

"I call it the crowd pleaser."

"Crowd pleaser?" Mullins asked? "It's a fucking canon, Taylor."

"Well, I have to compensate for something."

"And what is that?" Mullins asked.

"Never you mind," she said.

The troopers checked each other's appearance, and then knocked on the enormous door. Taylor tried knocking once more but to no avail.

"You kidding me?" she said. "Someone's just got to be there."

Just as they were about to check the back door, the door slowly opened and a small figure appeared. "Can I help you?" he asked.

"Yes, I'm Investigator Taylor and this is Mullins," she said as they flashed their badges quickly. "We are doing our preliminary investigation."

"Are you here in reference to the break-ins?" he asked.

"Sorry, sir, I didn't get your name," Mullins added.

"I did not give it," he said back rudely. "Well, if you must know, my name is Smithers, third-generation mortician.

Taylor couldn't help but look at this guy. His hair was so neatly cropped it really did remind her of an old-fashioned English butler. She found herself counting the oddly colored liver spots on his head.

"Err, break-ins?" she asked.

"Yes. The sheriff did not tell you about the break-ins?" he asked cautiously.

"No, but why don't you tell us," Taylor said.

"Could we come in?" Mullins interrupted.

"I am kind of busy, you see," Smithers fired back.

"Look, Mr. Smithers," Taylor said, seeing that Smithers was getting annoyed, "if you can tell us a little about the break-ins we will be out of your way."

"Well, come in," he said, opening the large door and leading them to the front hallway. "Please wait here," he said in a pompous tone. As he walked away, Mullins couldn't help but ridicule his demeanor to Taylor.

"Knock it off, Mullins," Taylor said. "Try not to screw this up. We really need this." She insisted they learn who was trying to get into the morgue, and why this could be the most important lead so far. "So get serious," she whispered as they watched Smithers walk back to them. He had a deliberate sense about him, sort of an *I'm better than you* air to himself. In his hands he was carrying a set of video tapes.

"Here," Smithers said as he shoved them into Taylor's hands. "Maybe these will help," he said. "Now I really must get back to work."

"Well, thank you for your time," Taylor said respectfully.

As they exited the morgue, Taylor had a great suspicion that the reason why the sheriff did not tell them anything about the break-ins was because he had something to hide, but what? Well, at least they had the tapes.

"Let's go see why the good sheriff did not tell us about the morgue break-ins. Hey, Mullins," Taylor said.

"What's up, boss?" Mullins returned.

"You hungry?"

"Funny," Mullins replied, "very funny."

Chapter 5

Fatal Error

Michael and Jenny hustled to get the rest of Jenny's personal items together.

"Shit," Jenny said.

"Look, only grab the essential items," Michael said.

"What about food?" Jenny asked.

"Jenny, we are leaving town not going on vacation." Michael said as he looked at Jenny's luggage. "Christ, Jenny, we got to leave, and leave right now."

As Michael grabbed the duffel bag from the bed he motioned Jenny to stop her movement. Jenny froze in her stance. Only her eyes followed Michael as he tiptoed to the door. He eased up to the door like a thief tiptoeing, ready to pounce. He skillfully edged up to the door and slowly peeped out. He almost jumped at what he found, for behind the door was none other than Sheriff Little. Yes, Sheriff Little had returned to the scene of the crime, so to speak. He knew for a fact that behind that door was at least one loose end that he had to tie. The sheriff, stout in figure, stood innocently behind Jenny's door and rattled the door knob.

"Err, Jenny! Jenny, you in there? I know you're in there," he added.

The sheriff continued to rattle the doorknob. His immense silhouette shadow looked intimidating. It looked like the sheriff wished he could force that lock. Michael motioned to Jenny to stay put as he continued to peep, hoping that the sheriff would just leave. It was like they both had a guardian angel for they heard a muffled, distorted noise.

Yes, it was dispatch, and they were asking the sheriff his location. The sheriff paused, and said he was out by the old cedar saw mill.

"That piece of shit," Michael muttered under his breath.

The distorted reply came back, asking the sheriff to respond to police headquarters to speak with Investigator Mullins. Michael eased his ears up against the door only to hear the sheriff say, "Shit."

Well, that was great news for Jenny and Michael. As they hustled out of the door, Jenny asked if Michael had any money.

"I got enough to get us the hell out of here," Michael replied.

They cautiously made their exit only to find a tow truck towing Michael's stolen car. *Well, how long it was going to stay stolen?* He shrugged his shoulders.

"What now?" he asked.

"We could take my car," Jenny said.

"Well, your car's kind of hot right now," Michael said.

"Hot," Jenny replied, "yes, hot. And we really don't need any more heat coming down on us."

"Look, Jenny," Michael said, as he turned to her. "I promise I'll fix this if it's the last thing I do. You got any change?" he asked. Jenny rummaged through her purse and handed Michael a few tarnished quarters.

"What are you doing?" Jenny asked.

"Just giving the sheriff a little payback," he replied.

Indeed, this was exactly what Michael had planned, to place an anonymous call to the sheriff's department, but not before notifying the media. This plan would have gone off great, without a hitch, but the sheriff had already dirtied his name, his entire character. Yet Michael thought to himself, *There must be some ray of hope out there.* He reached for the receiver of a public phone, which was by far the smelliest he'd used. It reeked of piss. he grabbed the receiver and wiped the ear and mouthpiece repeatedly, and then carefully dialed information, he listened as the phone rang, and a semi-aged voice cackled on the other end.

"Yes, um, I would like the phone number to the state police in Larit."

"Please hold for the number, the automated voice responded.

As Michael patiently waited he turned and looked at Jenny. She was definitely a special person.

Just then a voice came on the other end. "Hello," said Investigator Mullins.

"Yes," Michael stated, "I would like to talk to someone, anyone but Sheriff Little."

"Who is this?" Mullins asked.

"Look," Michael said, sounding irritated. If you want firsthand goods on the sheriff you will meet me here."

"Well, OK," Michael said, feeling he had gotten his point across. He went on to plan a meeting.

* * *

Taylor folded the paper and chewed on the tip of a No. 2 pencil. She really wanted this collar, not just for closure but to chalk one up for the state police. Mulllins was busy viewing the tape and Taylor was to meet Sheriff Little—so what better time to get the ball rolling and meet with this mystery person? Mullins was very excited, not only for a break in the case, but to be able to get the hell out of Larit. He missed his life back in the big city of Detroit, where he had solved numerous cases from behind his desk. Yes, this was the first time he was ever in the field. Sure he was able to get by pushing the pencil, but this was different, he thought to himself. This was a lot more dangerous. If Taylor and he could prove the sheriff was dirty they would really have to watch their backs. Yet a lead was a lead, and he was not going to let this one get away. He grabbed his jacket and headed toward the door, still watching Taylor as she seemed glued to the video tape, almost trance-like, trying to piece together this whole mess.

He motioned to her that he was just stepping out. She never responded. It always seemed that Investigator Taylor was married to her job. No kids, just a tough-looking female with her own style of femininity. He slowed down, to take a little glance at Taylor. After all, she really was not bad looking, he thought as he exited the office area and hustled out to meet Michael.

The sheriff pulled his police cruiser into the rear of the police parking lot. He was tired and hungry, but most of all he was pissed off that he did not get to see Jenny. At least with her out of the way he would have been able to focus on Michael. As he pulled into his assigned parking space he saw Mullins backing out and they made eye contact. Mullins tried to not let on, gave the sheriff a phony smile, and the sheriff returned one, revealing his dingy, coffee-stained teeth. As Mullins pulled out of the lot, the sheriff wondered where the hell he was off to. The sheriff was well aware that his chips were not falling where he wanted them to fall, and he was not going to be outwitted by some young punk passing through town. By far, everything was going the sheriff's way. The town was mobbed with media, just as he planned. The only thing he did not plan was that reporter. Yes, his thorn, his Achilles heel.

The sheriff exited his vehicle and walked through the maze of reporters camped outside. "Sheriff Little," one reporter asked, "any news on the sudden crime surge in Larit?"

"No comment," the sheriff said.

"Sheriff," one reporter said, "can you tell us about the disappearance of the diner owner?"

"Also, many more people have just disappeared," a reporter yelled.

The sheriff stopped in his tracks, and then turned to the flock of reporters. "Look," he said, "this has always been a quiet town. We've had our share of troublemakers but not like this. You have my word that when there's any break in this case you will be the first to know."

"Sheriff, do you have time for one more question?"

"Yes, what is it?" he asked.

"The suspect—we did a little research on him. He is out of New York."

"Yes, I know," the sheriff added.

"Well, it does not make any sense," the reporter said. "Why would he do these killings?"

"Sometimes people just snap," the sheriff said. "I really can't explain it," the sheriff fired back.

"But, sheriff, sheriff," the reporter added.

"That's enough. No more questions," the sheriff said.

The reporters yelled as the sheriff pushed his way through the gauntlet of reporters.

"Damn media," he muttered underneath his breath as he walked toward his office. He went to the coffee pot and shook his head, puzzled about the barrage of questions the reporters threw at him. He poured himself some coffee into his favorite mug and slowly savored the taste. Just then the door opened to the spare area that he had given to the state police and Investigator Taylor stood in the doorway.

"Tough crowd?" she asked.

"You bet," the sheriff said without turning toward her.

"Sheriff," Taylor said, "we visited the morgue this morning, and we had a few words with the attendant."

"Oh, Smithers," the sheriff interrupted.

"Yes, Smithers, a colorful guy."

The sheriff gestured.

"Yes, indeed," Taylor agreed. "You know, he is a third-generation mortician."

The sheriff said he knew.

Getting a little frustrated, Taylor said, "Sheriff, were you able to get any information out there?"

"Nothing," he said. "Everything seems to lead to a dead end."

"I was wondering, did Smithers ever mention anything to you about break-ins?" Taylor asked.

"Hmm, let me see. I remember him telling me something, but I did not take it too seriously," the sheriff said.

"May I ask why not?" Taylor asked.

"Listen, Taylor," the sheriff said as he finally turned to face her. "I have been the sheriff here for over thirty years and I don't need your kind telling me how to do my job."

"Remember, you called us in on this, sheriff," Taylor added.

"Yes, I did," the sheriff said, "but only to assist me and my men, not to run around town doing your own thing."

"And I was just trying to help."

"I know what you were trying to do," the sheriff said, interrupting rudely. "Listen, this is my town and what I say goes. That goes for you, your partner, and any other agency around here."

The sheriff stepped closer to Taylor and said, "You don't want to cross me. This is a small town and stranger shit has happened before." He leaned into her.

"Am I supposed to be afraid, sheriff?" Taylor asked, looking intently into his bloodshot eyes.

"No, just caution to the wise," he said, "just caution." He drank the last of his coffee and placed the dirty cup upside down. He then put his wide-brimmed hat on his head and said, "You have a good day," and he walked out of the office area.

What an asshole, Taylor thought as she followed him out of the office with her eyes. Still, she thought, she had gotten exactly what she wanted out of the sheriff.

* * *

Michael and Jenny waited patiently, hoping that all of the madness would come to an end. They were both tired and just wanted to get on with their lives. Jenny knew for sure that Michael was for her. She felt very secure as they waited patiently for the investigator to get to them. Unfortunately, the weather was changing for the worse.

"We should go," Jenny said as she tugged on Michael's arm.

"Just be patient," he said as he took the wool scarf that he was wearing and placed it around Jenny's neck. "Here. This should at least keep your neck warm."

She gazed amicably at Michael. "Wait, Michael," she said as he watched a vehicle get closer. "Be careful."

Michael parted the bushes where they were waiting for Mullins as the vehicle slowly came to a halt. Michael cautiously stood in place, wondering if this investigator was on the up-and-up. Mullins was no street cop, for sure. Michael read him as he exited the unmarked police vehicle.

"You Mullins?" Michael asked with a hint of caution in his voice.

"Yeah, you Michael?" Mullins responded.

"In the flesh."

"You know I am supposed to slap the cuffs on you and haul your ass right in," Mullins said.

"You do that and you will never solve these mystery murders."

"They are not murders yet, just simple case of sudden missing persons."

"Well, investigator," Michael said . . .

"Call me Mullins. You want to tell me what's going on?"

"Your guess is as good as mine," Michael replied. "All I know is that the sheriff has a stake in all the happenings."

"Really? Mullins said with more interest.

"Yeah, some freaky shit has been happening," Michael said.

"What can you tell me about the diner?" Mullins asked.

"The diner. Where do you want me to start? Michael replied.

"You ate their before?" Mullins asked.

"Yeah, the house special is the winner."

"I can imagine," Mullins said as his stomach growled.

"You OK?"

"Yeah," Mullins said, "just a little nauseous."

"You sure? Because what I have to tell you, you won't like," Michael said.

"Go for it."

As Michael began to tell his story to Mullins, Jenny, feeling that it was safe, came out from behind the hiding spot.

"Who's this? No, don't tell me," Mullins said. "Jenny, right?

"Yes," she said innocently.

"You know the entire town is looking for you," Mullins said like a caring parent. "Well, finish your story," he said to Michael.

As Michael continued to tell Mullins his findings, Mullins listened with great disbelief. But deep in the back of Mullins' head he knew that Michael was telling the truth. Yes, for he had firsthand knowledge that the diner was serving a special menu and the beef brisket was none other than boiled body parts sautéed in the house special sauce.

Michael went on explaining. As he continued, Mullins doubled over and started to vomit.

"Is he going to be OK? Jenny asked.

They watched as Mullins continued to spew his stomach all over the gravel.

"Well," Jenny said, "what now? Will he be able to help us?"

They turned and looked at Mullins who looked as if he was going to snap his neck as he continued to throw up his stomach contents.

"Please bear with me," Mullins insisted. "I will be right there."

"Oh, please take your time," Michael said sarcastically.

Mullins finally managed to get himself together. Then he said, "I have to find a way to get you back."

"Wait a minute," Michael said. "We had a deal."

"Deal!" Mullins said surprised. "You're lucky I don't haul your ass in."

"Michael," Jenny said.

"Wait, Jenny"

"Michael," she said again, "you promised our safety."

"Look," Mullins said, "we could do this the easy way or the hard way."

Just as Mullins started to reach for his cuffs he heard a familiar voice, and it wasn't just any voice. It was a voice that he had heard before. And he had grown to loathe it.

"Looks like you have a problem there."

Hearing this, Mullins spun around to see Sheriff Little standing there with his arms crossed.

"What we have here" the sheriff added, "is a breakdown in communication. You see, I am the sheriff of this town and I thought I made it clear that anything, and I mean anything, you find, I was to be notified. Now what am I supposed to do?" the sheriff asked.

Mullins, still confused at seeing the sheriff, said, "I, I don't quite understand."

"What you have there is our suspect," Sheriff Little added.

"Now, hold on, sheriff. I was going to bring him in. You know, for questioning."

"Questioning!" the sheriff said with a laugh. "What the hell were you going to question him about? He's a cop killer."

"Cop killer?" Mullins said in bewilderment.

"Yeah, cop killer."

Sheriff Little reached for his chrome-plated 357 magnum. Mullins, still in shock, still stood there, his feet unable to move, as if they were one with the gravel road. He watched his entire life flash before him.

"Naanoo!!" Mullins yelled and tried to reach for his service weapon. His slow reaction and his shock made him certain that he was about to die.

Mullins pulled out his service weapon. Any chance was better than no chance. The first shot rang through the morning air, surprising a flock of crows that showed their displeasure by flapping their wings violently. With this, Michael and Jenny—not wanting to get in the crossfire—started to run. The second shot rang out as Mullins lay half dead. Mullins still had a look of surprise as Sheriff Little knelt down beside him. Mullins was choking on his own blood.

Mullins whispered to the sheriff, "You, you bastard."

"Hey, that's Mr. Bastard," the sheriff said as he stuck the muzzle close to the rib cage of the slowly dying trooper. "This is my town, and don't you forget it."

The sheriff stood there, making sure that Mullins was down. Then he gingerly walked over to his cruiser and screamed, "Officer down!! Officer down!!" With this, dispatch frantically relayed the message as the sheriff walked back over to Mullins' corpse and coolly put on some gloves. He then reached for Mullins' unfired weapon and fired two shots, one toward the wooded area and the other striking his squad car. Yes, he was to stage the scene just right. Then he took Mullins' weapon and placed it inside a dark bag.

Investigator Taylor was at the police station, still numb from the apparent ass chewing she had received from the sheriff. "What a jerk," she muttered to herself as she reached for her cell phone, and tried to contact Mullins. "Damnit," she said, redialing his phone number. "Mullins, where are you?" she said as she got ready to leave a message.

She stood by the station radio room, where she ultimately heard the sheriff's screams for help. Instinct told her to just go. She grabbed her vest, which was lying on the chair, and darted out of the office, only to be cut off by another Larit officer trying to go to the sheriff's aid. As she got into her vehicle she had a gut feeling that something was wrong. She lit a cigarette, inhaled deeply, and spun the vehicle around. "Shit, Mullins," she muttered. She knew for a split second that when Mullins had not checked in, something was wrong, yes, terribly wrong. She sped off in a frantic state.

Jenny and Michael were tired, scared, worn out and confused.

"If only Investigator Mullins had believed me," Michael said as he spat on the floor.

"The sheriff," Jenny said, "the damn sheriff killed that man in cold blood."

"Yes, he did," Michael said. "We have to get out of this town, and now.

"What will we do?" Jenny asked. "What will we do?"

"I don't know," Michael said. "Just let me think." He stood there, oblivious to the fact that they had covered a considerable amount of territory in a short amount of time.

"We are fucked," Jenny said.

"I would think so," Michael said.

"By now, every gun-toting law enforcement officer—state and local—will be looking for us," Jenny said.

"Yeah," Michael said. "You really think the sheriff will not implicate you, too? This man would try anything and I mean anything to get us."

"Why do you think he didn't chase us?" Jenny wondered aloud.

"C'mon, Jenny, we've got to go," Michael said as he stretched out his hand for Jenny's.

"Michael," Jenny said, "the cops are looking for a couple. Why don't we split up?"

"You sure you want to go that route?" Michael asked in surprise. "You know, with the sheriff out there, you will not stand a chance in hell of surviving."

"Yes," Jenny said, "but we must try."

Michael looked into her eyes, still blinded with tears. Her face told a different story, a story of fear, dejection and just plain fear. Michael felt very bad for getting her involved. It just happened. He did not plan to fall in love but he was smitten.

"Look," Michael said he as he gazed into her eyes, "the next time we have a chance to really split, we split. Until then we stay together."

With this they continued to flee through the wooded terrain.

The town again was abuzz with excitement. Even more news media had arrived and amid the confusion, one investigator found herself very frustrated yet hardened at the death of her partner. She kept on seeing the images of Mullins just lying there cold and helpless. Knowing what kind of person Mullins was, she figured he did not have time to react. Not complacent; just Mullins being Mullins. "Always the cop, and not the hero," Taylor said to herself.

Taylor asked the ambulance crew where they were taking the body.

"Err, to the morgue until his next of kin can be notified," the driver said.

Taylor, knowing what kind of hellhole the morgue was, told them to leave that to her, that she would take care of this one. Taylor felt that was the least that she could do. She was to send her partner back alone, dead. She felt like it was her fault for not being there for him.

She turned away from the ambulance and started to walk toward her cruiser. Her walk was interrupted by the sheriff.

"Pity about your partner," he said, sounding almost cynical. "I am sure he did not suffer."

"You know this for sure?" Taylor asked, turning to him.

"I know that that son of a bitch almost hit me."

"You, you were here?" Taylor asked with a quizzical look on her face.

"Sure," Sheriff Little said. "I happened to come upon them when that boy there overpowered Mullins and shot him. Yeah, close range. He said he figured you would pack up shop and go back to your department."

Taylor turned and slowly walked toward the sheriff. "Listen, I was sent to this shit hole you call a town to investigate the disappearance of certain people. Now the gloves are off," Taylor said. "Now it's time for me to show this town who is the bigger bitch."

"Whoa, whoa there, darling," the sheriff said, pushing his dirty palms up.

Taylor, as smart as she was, noticed that the sheriff had residue marks on his wrists and quickly turned her focus away.

"Look," the sheriff added, "we know for sure they are still at large. They have nowhere to go. We have an interstate dragnet in progress. How far can they get?"

"Yeah," Taylor said, "how far? Looks like we have us a modern-day Bonnie and Clyde." She brushed past the sheriff and noticed that his gun was missing. *Funny,* she thought, *a sheriff without a gun? Never go to a gun battle without a gun, no matter what,* she thought as she turned toward the sheriff.

"I am sorry," she said. "I guess I just got caught up in the moment,"

"Hey, hey," the sheriff said, "you have every right to feel this way. We will get them and when we do, I promise, you will be the first to know."

I bet I will be, she thought to herself. *I bet I will.*

* * *

Chapter 6

Timing is Everything

The bad weather had somewhat subsided. Michael and Jenny kept on walking, not knowing where exactly they were going.

"How are your feet?" Michael asked Jenny.

"Not that bad. How about yours?"

Michael tried his best to sound brave. "Oh, me—I'm fine. You hungry? he asked Jenny.

"Boy," she said, "if I was back at the diner, I would make us a juicy steak."

"Huh," Michael said.

"Yeah, with all the trimmings, the works," she said.

As they continued to walk, they saw a ray of hope coming toward them.

"It's a car," Jenny said with excitement.

"Look, Jenny," Michael said, "we don't know who is in that vehicle."

"Still," Jenny said, "this just may be our ride out of here. Anything is better than freezing our asses off."

"You go," Michael said to her. "You go."

As the vehicle got closer, they could hear the driver singing. Jenny stood by the road and waved the vehicle down. As the vehicle came to a full stop, Michael couldn't see the driver well, but it must of gone well, he thought to himself. Jenny slyly turned to his direction and whispered *I love you* as she got into the vehicle, which was a relief to Michael. *Well, at least she will be safe,* he thought as he watched the vehicle slowly disappear into the evening horizon.

He turned up the collar on his jacket and continued to walk, feeling like he was walking in vain. He played different scenarios in his head—what ifs, so to speak. He had come to Larit as a reporter just passing through, and now he was labeled cop killer and abductor. He was once heralded in New York as one of the best investigative reporters around. Now he felt dejected, worn out, almost ready to throw in the towel. Yet he pushed on.

He felt the darkness swallow him up, and he felt as if he was just walking aimlessly—only because he was. He smiled to himself, hoping that Jenny's departure from town would save his skin, especially when Jenny witnessed Mullins' murder. Things were definitely changing, Michael thought to himself. Instead of clearing his name he was determined to get the hell out of Dodge. He continued walking. With every cold step he felt a little more at ease, knowing that Jenny was not going to be part of this mess. He smiled to himself.

Taylor was having a hell of a night. She spent most of it trying to piece together what may or did happen. *Still,* she thought to herself, *did it matter?* She turned toward the television and listened to Sheriff Little give his version of the tragic shoot-out, which had left an investigator dead. As she listened intently, it seemed quite odd that Sheriff Little happened to be there at that specific location. She couldn't quite get it. No.

She wondered why her partner did not call her. She gazed out the cruiser and then opened the glove compartment to get her cell phone. She saw that it said one missed called. When she scrolled down, it said Mullins. She immediately started to weep, for she knew if she had answered her phone he might still be alive. She took a deep breath and headed back to town. While driving, she kept playing different scenarios over in her head. "Enough," she said to herself. "I must stay strong, and I must take that son of a bitch down."

The sheriff had been very busy, drawing attention away from himself. The only person who knew about his dealings was Smithers. Yes, how was he to deal with Smithers, that double-crossing bastard, he thought to himself. He parked his vehicle at the back of the morgue, knowing that his position as sheriff was the perfect cover. He had a knack for killing. Yes, the sheriff did. The post-war stress syndrome had nothing on him. He took off his hat and poured hot coffee from his thermos. He wondered how he was going to dispose of Smithers and sat back thinking to himself, *retirement here I come.* He had had enough of the town of Larit. He had definitely made his mark. Things were becoming a little too hot. He had put in a lot of work since he arrived, getting rid of the riffraff, decapitating them, then selling the parts back to the unsuspecting diner owner. His plan was lucrative—as well as tasty. Now he would set up shop somewhere else, possibly a small, unassuming town like Larit. Yes, he was on to gold, he thought to himself, as he backed up slowly, turned his lights off, and began his stakeout of the morgue.

Investigator Taylor knew exactly what she had to do. She had followed all the leads that she and Mullins had, yet everything they had came back, full circle, to the sheriff. She dared not question the sheriff's underlings for fear of reprisal. She knew the only lead she had was the video tape that Smithers, however weird, had given her. She would go and question Smithers, she thought to herself as she pulled a small writing pad from her jacket pocket, and scribbled his name messily on the paper. She really wished that she could have made contact with one or both of the suspects in the morgue break-ins. That would have shed some light. She placed the writing pad back into her jacket pocket, and started the long task of getting back to the morgue, hoping to see Smithers, for she felt like Smithers was trying to send her a message.

As she drove past the wooded area, she reached down to get a cigarette. Ordinarily, she would not smoke. Actually, she had thought about quitting; however, given the turnabout of things, she welcomed that familiar taste of nicotine as she took a very long draw from her cigarette. "Wow," she said to herself, feeling totally light-headed. The smoke from the cigarette filled the vehicle, and she tried desperately to fan the smoke away. As she did this, she carelessly started to swerve, veering from one lane to the next, and fearing an accident. She quickly brought the vehicle to a grinding halt. "Shit," she said as she flipped her auburn hair back and dived into her purse, hoping to find an elastic band to tie her hair back into a ponytail. She neatly grasped a handful of hair, and twisted it, ready to put it into a ponytail. She expertly placed a rubber band into her mouth and adjusted her rearview mirror to fix her hair. She saw that her eyes were slightly bloodshot from crying. "Shit," she said. "What a mess."

She adjusted the mirror, easily bringing it down to her eye level. As she did this, she looked to her left, and her right. She quickly tied her hair, and reached for her weapon, just for her safety. She thought there was too much freaky shit happening. As she exited her vehicle she felt an uninvited presence was there with her.

She slowly unholstered her weapon and said, "Who's there!!" She was normally calm and cool but this was different. "Police!!" she yelled as she walked toward the wooded area. She pointed her weapon toward a dark silhouetted shadow.

"Please, please don't shoot," a scared voice yelled from the darkness.

"Listen to me," Taylor ordered. "Walk out slowly toward the sound of my voice. Do it now."

"Please, just don't shoot me."

Taylor continued barking her orders as Michael, hungry and wet, walked out of the thickly wooded area. He just wanted to spill his story. He really did not care who was out there; he had to tell somebody, anybody who would just listen to him.

"That's far enough," Taylor yelled at him. "Keep your hands high and turn around with your back to me and walk toward my voice."

Michael did this, because the one thing he feared was catching a hot shell in his ass.

"Turn to me, slowly," Taylor yelled. "Do it, and do it now!" she commanded.

Michael slowly turned, complying with her every command.

"Sir, stop!" she yelled, "right now, slowly, palms out. Face the floor."

"What floor?" Michael yelled back. "It is nothing but dead weed and shit."

With this Michael received a pain-wrenching kick to the back.

"And stay down," she said as she quickly frisked and cuffed him.

"What's going on?" Michael asked.

"Keep your mouth shut!" she screamed.

"I, I did nothing," Michael said. "I was framed."

"Framed. I guess you were framed, too, for killing that cop," she hissed at Michael.

Michael, now fearing for his life, pleaded, "Please, listen to me. It was the sheriff. It was the sheriff."

There was a slight pause in the barrage of accusations from Taylor. "Wait," she said, "you know for sure that Sheriff Little pulled the trigger?"

"Yes," he said, "yes, it was him. I saw him gun down that poor officer. The officer had no chance in hell. Sheriff Little came from behind, surprising him. I, I saw everything."

"Everything," Taylor echoed, lowering her weapon and easing her finger away from the trigger.

She cautiously walked toward Michael, whose face was bruised from the weeds and bushes. He looked defeated as tears streamed down his face. He tried to wipe his tears with his shoulder.

"You were going to kill me," he said to Taylor.

"If I wanted to kill you," she said, "you would be dead. I guess your story seems believable."

"You're darn right," Michael said, gaining confidence. "Well, can you take off the cuffs?"

"Listen, even though I believe you, you are still a wanted person."

"Wanted, yes," Michael said, "guilty, no. Look, just get me out of here, and I will testify. I will tell the world. Just get me out of this crazy town."

"Yeah, and stay away from the diner," Taylor added.

"You mean, you know?" Michael said, surprised,

"Yes," Taylor said. "Poor Mullins had a firsthand experience."

"Yeah, and I know where the meat supply comes from," Michael said with confidence—the morgue."

"No shit," Taylor said.

"Now can you take these cuffs off?" Michael asked.

"The cuffs stay on," she said, helping him to his feet.

"Thanks," he said.

"Look, I am sorry if I treated you a bit harshly back there," Taylor said.

"I understand completely," Michael said.

"We need to get to the morgue. If only we had physical proof," Taylor said.

"Proof? I am not going back there. No way," Michael said.

"It's the only way I can get you out of this mess, if only I can talk to Smithers."

"Oh, you mean the butler-looking guy?"

"Yeah, him," Taylor said. "Look, we need to get you to a safe spot, anyplace but Larit."

“If we do pull this off,” Michael said, “we can get the sheriff,” Taylor said cheerfully.

“Good ol’ Sheriff Little,” Michael said as Taylor stood behind him and held his arm.

“If we get that information, I promise you, the only thing that will stick is the breaking and entering charge.”

“OK,” Michael said.

“One thing at a time,” Taylor said as she opened the door to her cruiser. “Get in.”

She gently guided his head into the vehicle. Deep in her heart she knew that Michael was telling the truth, yet he was a suspect. Dirty or not, she had her own rules. She had lost one good partner and she was certain that good old Sheriff Little would be waiting for her with his pretentious grin, showing his discolored teeth, and his know-it-all persona. Yes, this time she would deal with him her way.

“What now?” Michael asked.

“Well,” Taylor replied, looking back in her rearview mirror, “we need to get you to safety.”

“I am all out of ideas,” Michael said with a bit of anxiety.

“Yeah. Me, too,” Taylor said.

Well, I am not going back to the police station.”

“You crazy?” Taylor snapped. “Those boys will surely skin you alive. You don’t kill a cop and then just turn yourself in. I guess you are stuck with me.”

“Yeah, just my luck,” Michael replied as they sped off in the direction of the morgue, hoping to get that oh, so ever-crucial statement from Smithers.

In a way, Smithers could actually seal the fate of the sheriff, she thought. She felt like she was alone in a small little world with no one to come to her rescue. She felt bad, bad for Mullins, and even worse for Michael. His entire reputation was soiled.

“You got family? she asked.

“Family? Michael asked.

“Look, just trying to make simple conversation, said Taylor.

“Well, let’s see, Michael said, “I have been on the lam ever since I got here. This place. I, I just don’t get it,” Michael said, raising his voice. “It’s just strange.”

“Hey, calm down, good buddy,” Taylor said.

"Please don't humor me," Michael said.

"Just let me do the planning, and together we might just beat that son of a bitch," Taylor said.

Michael smirked in agreement as Taylor continued to speed in the direction of the morgue.

The night seemed unusually chilly. The leafless trees stood erect like frozen black figurines, lining the roadway. The icy wind bellowed through the trees like a pressured whistle ready to blow. It seemed as if the wind was gently talking to the rustling fallen leaves.

The sheriff was still waiting like a hungry predator, lurking wantonly, ready to pounce. Poor Smithers. The sheriff chuckled to himself as he sat in his cruiser contemplating how he would approach Smithers. Smithers was definitely on the sheriff's side; Smithers just went along with the program. Whose program? Sheriff Little's program. But now the sheriff thought Smithers was more of a liability than a comrade. The sheriff would deal with him just as he had dealt with his other problems. He relished the thought of disposing of Smithers, that baldheaded fuck. The sheriff turned off his parking lights as he saw a vehicle approaching the morgue.

"I don't mean to rude," Michael said, "but I really can't feel my arms, and I have to . . ."

"I know, I know. You got to pee," Taylor said, finishing his sentence.

As they pulled into the parking lot of the morgue, Taylor turned her lights off. "What about me?" Michael asked.

"I guess I can give you the benefit of the doubt," she said as she reached into her pocket to retrieve her handcuff key. She suddenly heard a raspy voice.

"Don't you have anything better to do than sneak around here?"

It was Smithers.

Taylor jumped back in her seat, reaching for her weapon on instinct.

"Damn it, Smithers," she barked. "You trying to give me a heart attack?"

"Surely not, ma'am," he said gently. "I had some work to do so I thought I would catch up, so to speak."

Smithers peeped into the back of the cruiser.

"Forgive me, ma'am. I'm not being rude but surely that's the gentleman who visited the morgue after hours."

"Yes it's me, you rude bastard," Michael said.

"I take it you two already met."

"Yeah, sort of," Michael responded.

"Here, let me help you," Taylor said as she helped Michael remove the cuffs.

"Thanks, Michael said as he rubbed each wrist. "Those cuffs were digging into me."

"They are not made for comfort," Taylor said. "Smithers, can we speak inside?"

"Yes," he said, "but very briefly."

Smithers led them into the graceful hallway.

"You were saying, ma'am?"

"Look, Smithers, I know you are involved in this mess. You either come clean or I will bust your ass for obstruction.

Smithers' face immediately turned a glossy red. "Surely you can't be saying that I have anything to do with those bodies," he said.

"What bodies, Smithers?" Taylor said cunningly.

"Oh, dear," he said. "Please, if I do divulge what I know, will you spare me the embarrassment?"

That was the all he said. Poor Smithers did not get to finish his sentence because a loud shot rang out.

"Smithers," Taylor said.

His once proud body lay slumped on the floor.

"You have got to be kidding me," Michael said. "It is everywhere I turn. Someone always end up dead."

"You stay here," Taylor said as she crouched down, taking a battle stance. "I have a dirty sheriff to bag."

With this, Taylor eased her way, trying to find the light. She had to do this for the sheriff had the upper hand. He was able to easily pick off Smithers with his high-powered sniper rifle. His advantage was the cover of night.

"Smart son of a bitch," Taylor whispered as she crawled low, toward the light switches, turning them off.

The sheriff was feeling more confident. He was definitely a good shot. He carefully picked up his rifle, and proceeded to walk toward the morgue. He knew that no one but Smithers and Michael could implicate him, and now he had them and Taylor where he wanted them. This would be too easy, he thought as he edged toward the basement window. He gave it a great kick, shattering the glass into splinters.

"Shit" he said, "I must be getting old."

He climbed through the morgue's basement window.

Now Taylor, still very cautious in the big building, had to take her time. She had no flashlight, so she had to rely on her police training,

"You should have stayed away, bitch." It was the sheriff. "I tried giving you a nice subtle warning but, no, you did not listen.

As a shot rang out, Taylor was still confused at how the sheriff's voice seemed so very close. Still crouched and gripping her weapon, Taylor screamed out, "You killed Mullins!" She fired, aiming into the darkness,

"You came close," the sheriff said, "but no cigar."

The sheriff fired another shot.

"You and that nosey reporter—you just couldn't leave well alone."

The sheriff again fired a shot. The round definitely ricocheted off an unfixed object, sending it crashing to the floor.

"Gee," Taylor said, "for a sheriff, you sure suck firing back again into darkness."

"If only I could get my hands around your fucking neck, cunt!" the sheriff screamed. He was now becoming very agitated.

"You will what," Taylor teased him, "eat me? You fucking sicko."

As Michael listened he was scared shitless and wondered if he was dreaming, for surely here were two cops firing at each other while having a fucking conversation. This really couldn't have happened to anyone but him, he thought, trying his best to tiptoe to the door.

Another shot rang out.

"Not so fast," the sheriff said as he fired a round, grazing Michael's neck.

"Shit! Damnit, Michael, I told you to stay put," Taylor yelled.

"Yeah, Michael," the sheriff taunted him, "I will be coming for you next, as soon as I dispose of this here problem."

The sheriff again fired into the dark.

"Shit, Taylor, we are not getting anywhere. Why don't you show yourself and we can just end this right here, right now."

"Oh, I bet you would like that, sheriff, wouldn't you? Tell me, how long did you think this would go on?" Taylor asked.

"Bitch, as long as it took."

The sheriff then tried to fire a round. *Click. Click. Click.* His weapon was empty.

Hearing this, Taylor carefully walked toward the incessant clicking.

"Damnit," the sheriff said.

"You will kill no more," Taylor said as she raised her weapon. "Good-bye, sheriff."

Then a click.

"Hello, bitch," the sheriff said as he punched her squarely in her face. Her body seemed to tell her one thing yet her persistent courage and true grit said another.

"You hit like a bitch," Taylor said, wiping her mouth and spitting the blood to the floor. "You killed my partner."

She placed a perfect kick to the sternum of the already stunned sheriff.

Little doubled over in agony and said, "Is that all . . . you got?"

Taylor squared her shoulders, paused and said, "Now, you GO TO HELL!!"

She thrust a large piece of broken glass into his jugular and thick blood oozed from his neck. Gurgling blood, the sheriff just stood still with a look of disbelief in his eyes. He fell to his knees, still looking at Taylor, who said to him, "Now stay dead, you bastard," as the sheriff gasped his last breath in pain. Taylor stood over him, in victory. Michael, having seen enough, gently slipped away, wandering aimlessly into the wintry night.

* * *

"And that's exactly how I met you," Michael said to Oswald.

"Wow, what a story!" Oswald said in disbelief."

"Yeah," Michael said, "I know."

The End